...But he realized he was back in his old body and the laugh turned into a hacking, coughing, old man's laugh that lasted for a good thirty ticks of his clock before he finally stopped.

"You want to know where I was?" he asked Dot, who had rolled her wheelchair closer to his bed.

She nodded.

Saber remembered the pitched fight he'd just had with six alien pirates, the success they had had again in defending the *Earth Protection League* and its space.

"You won't believe me, but I would love to tell you."

"You never know what I might believe," she said.

He laughed softly this time, avoiding the hacking cough.

He couldn't believe it. After all the years of going out and coming back, of defending earth against all odds, and all alien scum, he *finally* got to tell someone.

And for the next hour it felt wonderful.

Almost as good as killing those alien pirates.

Almost.

Life of a Dream
Copyright © 2018 Dean Wesley Smith
First published in a different form in Smith's Monthly #8, *May 2014*
Published by WMG Publishing
Cover and Layout copyright © 2018 by WMG Publishing
Cover design by Allyson Longueira/WMG Publishing
Cover art copyright © innovari/Depositphotos
ISBN-13: 978-1-56146-610-8
ISBN-10: 1-56146-610-7

LIFE OF A DREAM

AN EARTH PROTECTION LEAGUE NOVEL

DEAN WESLEY SMITH

PUBLISHING

For Kris
Who is putting up with me getting older between every mission

AUTHOR'S NOTE

Early parts of this novel are new and altered variations of four short stories. I liked how Brian and Dot's narrative evolved in the stories, so I decided to include them in altered form instead of telling them again. The four stories are: "The Gift of a Dream," "Hand and Space," "A Time to Dream," and "Dreams of a Moon."

PART ONE
THE FIRST MISSION

ONE

December 24th, 2018
Actual Earth Time
Location: Chicago

DOROTHY "DOT" LEEDS pulled herself slowly up to a sitting position, using the metal railing on her nursing home bed. The railing was cold in her hand and the room felt like it had a chill to it. She rubbed her old legs through her thin cotton nightgown, slowly, as if doing so would bring back some of the long, lost feeling to them. She had been dreaming again. Dreaming of dancing, as she and her husband used to do every Saturday night.

Like him, and most of the use of her legs, those days were long gone.

Yet every night, without fail, she dreamed of dancing. Usually the dream was of a small dance floor just big enough to swirl around. Often she was with her dead husband, Dave. Sometimes she was with a handsome man she couldn't exactly see clearly.

3

She could never really see the dancehall or who was watching around the edges. It was a dream and those people didn't matter.

Moving, dancing was all that was important. She loved the feeling of almost flying around the floor, the strong grip of her partner helping her float like a bird on a soft wind.

In this reality, at her advanced age, she was far from a bird in any form.

Around her, the Shady Valley Nursing Home was quiet.

The Christmas festive decorations filled the hall outside her open door, and later today she knew there'd be ham for Christmas Eve dinner. She had enjoyed that ham dinner for years now and actually looked forward to it, since the ham was always moist and soft and allowed her old teeth to chew it easily.

Then there would be turkey tomorrow for Christmas dinner. Sometimes they overcooked the turkey and it was tough, other times it had been moist and the dressing wonderful. The same two meals every Christmas for years now, since she had moved in here and her only son had moved from Chicago to the west coast and no longer took her out for Christmas or Christmas Eve dinners. Now he could only afford an occasional holiday call and a once-a-year summer visit.

She knew he felt bad about missing holidays, but her time was almost gone and he had a family to spend the holidays with and enjoy. He did what he could for her, she understood that. She didn't blame him at all and even had encouraged him to stay with his family at Christmas and let her enjoy her friends here.

She took a deep breath and kept rubbing her legs, slowly, trying to get any kind of feeling into them.

She could hear the faint ticking of Brian Saber's old wall clock across the hall, but nothing more.

It was now Christmas Eve day, very early in the morning actually, and for some reason, Christmas Eve always seemed to be quieter than any time of the year. Not even the snowstorm outside rattled the windows. The wind off Lake Michigan must have shifted as the weatherman on television earlier had predicted it would. It was amazing what people could do these days with science stuff.

She glanced at the blue numbers of her alarm clock. Two minutes after four in the morning.

"Oh, great, just great," she said softly to herself. It would be at least another hour before the night nurse stopped in to check on her. She was going to need to use the bathroom before then. That's what she got for having that second cup of tea. Now she was paying for it.

"Go slow," she whispered, talking to herself.

She rolled over and eased down the bar on the side of her bed, then levered herself slowly to the edge, and made sure her wheelchair was in position and the brake locked. Last thing she would need on Christmas Eve was that thing rolling away from her and her falling and breaking an old brittle bone.

Using the muscles in her stomach to control her legs, as she had taught herself to do twenty-five years ago after the car accident, she rolled on her side and moved her mostly dead legs off the edge of the bed. Then with a twist she had done hundreds of times, she half-dropped, half-lowered herself into her wheelchair.

She could still stand, still move her legs enough to shuffle, still walk in a very slow fashion with support and she did that as often as she could, but that took real focus and she felt better not trying to make it most places without sitting in the wheelchair.

Especially if she was alone like this.

The feeling of making it safely into the chair made her smile.

She often had the nurse or orderly help her out of bed just for safety, but still having the freedom to do it on her own was the most important thing she held onto.

At eighty-four years of age, freedom was everything. There sure wasn't much else.

She wheeled her chair around and headed for the bathroom.

She was halfway there when a cold draft whipped her nightgown around her legs, as if someone close by had opened a door.

Her sliding door led out to the front garden of the nursing home. It was closed and the drapes hung down limp. Her room's big metal door into the hallway was braced open as it always was at night.

She could see slightly in the faint light from the nurse's station and her nightlight in her bathroom. Nothing was out of place.

She must have imagined that or a ghost had drifted past her. So many people had died in this nursing home over the years, it wouldn't have surprised her if it was haunted.

She was about to continue on toward the restroom when she glanced out and across the hall.

There she saw a young man, shadowed and wearing some sort of dark uniform, pick eighty-five-year-old Brian Saber out of his bed and head for his room's sliding glass door. That door led outside into the cold winter night and the center courtyard of the nursing home.

There was nothing out there.

No one even went out there until the spring and summer and early fall.

At first she was stunned at what she saw.

"Get help, you idiot," she muttered. She was about to shout for the nurse when she heard Brian's distinctive laugh.

Whatever was happening, Brian was a part of it. He didn't seem to be minding at all.

Maybe it was some sort of Christmas gift from someone.

Maybe Brian's son was giving him a treat of some kind.

She knew he had one son, but they hadn't talked about him much at all, other than Brian was proud of him.

After a moment, the man carrying Brian had again opened the sliding door to Brian's room and the two of them had disappeared silently outside, leaving only a short draft of cold air behind as the door slid silently closed.

What in the world was Brian up to?

She talked with him a lot during lunches and dinners.

In fact, she considered him her best friend in the place, and if they had been younger by a few decades, she was sure they would have been having a fling, since Brian's wife had died about the same time as her husband.

Yet Brian had never mentioned doing anything like this. He seemed so down-to-earth, solid. Something crazy didn't make sense for him in her mind.

She waited, almost holding her breath in the silence of the nursing home night, then eased out into the hallway.

To her right was the bright-lit nurse's station, decorated in red ribbons and white bows. She could see the night-nurse's head sticking just above the top of the low counter. She was obviously bent over some paperwork and paying no attention at all.

Taking a deep breath, Dot silently wheeled her chair quickly the rest of the way across the hall and into Brian's room.

His bed was slept in, the blankets and sheet pushed back, his wheelchair beside his nightstand, his old wall clock ticked the seconds away.

But there was no sign of Brian.

She sat for a moment, listening to the wall clock count down the remaining time in her life.

This was so strange.

She moved to the sliding glass door that opened from his room out into a central courtyard. She pulled the curtain aside, not knowing what to expect.

There was nothing out there.

A cold Chicago night. She could almost feel the cold radiating through the glass to her thin skin. She shivered and moved closer to see where Brian had gone.

In the snow, she could see a man's tracks coming from the center of the courtyard to Brian's door, another set going back. But she couldn't see where they had gone.

Maybe through another door on the other side of the courtyard, but she had no idea why they would do that.

She had no idea why Brian would do any of this.

She eased her chair away from the window and moved it so she was sitting in the dark corner of the room.

She had a sneaking hunch Brian would be back very shortly. And she didn't plan on leaving until then, no matter how badly she needed to go to the bathroom.

TWO

December 24th, 1956
Equivalent Earth Time
Location: Deep Space

CAPTAIN BRIAN SABER of the *Earth Protection League* slapped the two hot Proton Stunners into their holsters on his hips, ran a hand through his thick head of wavy brown hair, and smiled at the six dead bodies of Bocturian scum.

"I don't think you'll be sabotaging any more slow-speed Earth supply ships."

They didn't answer, for obvious reasons.

They were dead.

He felt proud, staring at the oil-smelling bodies, their tentacles twitching in the air, their six eyes staring in their death stare. They looked like a bad cross between an octopus and a pile of dog crap.

Around him the control room of their ship stank of a combination of fish and intense lilac perfume. Brothel jokes were common anytime anyone from the *Earth Protection League* had to board a Bocturian ship.

He knew for a fact that it was going to take some time before the smell got out of his leather pants, silk shirt, leather vest, and high boots. He hoped it washed out before his next mission, otherwise his crew was never going to let him forget it.

One of the pirates seemed to move and he shot it again just for good measure.

"Captain?" Carl Turner, his third in command asked over the communications link. "Are you wrapped up there?"

"Bows are tied and presents under the tree," he said, kicking each pile of pirate scum to make sure it wasn't alive. "How about the rest of the Bocturian ships?"

In this mission there had been ten *Earth Protection League* ships fighting a small fleet of Bocturian pirates. The pirates hadn't stood a chance.

"Cleaned up," Turner said.

Saber felt a slight tinge of regret. The mission was almost over. "Prepare to pick me up," he ordered. "I'm going to need a good bath before we head back to Earth."

"I copy that," Turner said. "I can smell you from here."

"Next time you do the boarding," Saber said, laughing.

Damn it felt good to be alive and needed to defend Earth.

"Uh, Captain," Turner said, "we took a slight hit to the forward section of the ship."

"Anyone hurt?"

The twisting in Saber's gut told him the answer to his question. On this mission there had been only ten of them on the ship instead of the normal thirty-eight to forty-two crew. Sometimes the ship held up to fifty crew members, but they had needed only the gunners and support crew this time, since the mission had been easy and designed to be quick.

But Saber knew that two of that small crew had been in the forward section.

"Ben and Sarah," Turner said, his voice soft and low. "Ben will survive. Sarah was killed."

"Damn, damn, damn," Saber said.

He hadn't known Sarah that well, but she had a great smile and an infectious laugh. She had barely topped five feet tall, but seemed really tough. They had been on six missions together, with her working weapons for him on two of the last three. He didn't even know what part of Earth she was from, or how old she was back there. But if she did have some family, they weren't going to have a happy Christmas Eve.

"Inform command and medical," Saber said.

"Copy that," Turner said.

With one more kick at the closest of the dead pirates, Saber turned and headed for the airlock.

Twenty minutes later, after a quick shower, he was standing over the coffin-like bed of his sleep chamber.

He had already tossed his uniform into the cleaning bins to be laundered when they returned to Earth, and had pulled his nursing home nightshirt over his young body. It always felt weird doing that, yet he knew that on the other end of the flight having the nightshirt on was better than having one of the young soldiers dress him.

He sighed and stared at the sleep chamber. The problems with Trans-Galactic flight were the reasons he was here.

At top speeds, Trans-Galactic flight regressed a human body, so for T-G jumps to the outer limits of the *Earth Protection League* borders, they had to use old people to start.

He was just about as old as they came.

No one really understood exactly why T-G flight worked that way.

Or why on the return flight, they returned to their original age.

Or at least no one had been able to explain it to him in a way he understood. He knew it had something to do with relativity, the curved nature of space above the speed of light, all combined with the fixed nature of matter.

None of it made any sense to him.

All he knew was that on Earth he was an eighty-five-year-old cripple in a nursing home, trying to fight off more strokes. Out here on the borders of the *Earth Protection League* space, he was a young and healthy man again. All thanks to the nature of Trans-Galactic flight.

He climbed into the coffin-shaped sleep chamber and smoothed down his old nightshirt. Then with a sigh of resignation, he quickly pulled the lid down, triggering the departure and his quick nap.

Fighting the alien pirates had taken him three days out here. He'd be back in his room early Christmas Eve morning, less than twenty minutes after he had left.

But he'd still have the three days of fresh memories.

That was one of the good things about the relative nature of time and space and matter.

With luck, there'd be another mission this week.

And then he would have another chance to be young again, fight the good fight as a hero of the *Earth Protection League* on the very edges of civilized space.

THREE

December 24th, 2018
Actual Earth Time
Location: Chicago

THE YOUNG SOLDIER picked him out of the sleep chamber as if
he weighed nothing. Actually, he didn't weigh much more than a
hundred pounds these days. And he ate as much as he could, but
couldn't seem to put any weight on his old body.

"How'd the mission go, Captain?" the soldier asked as the tractor
beam released them in the center court of the nursing home and the
soldier moved with sure steps through the soft snow.

"Just about as good as could be hoped," Saber said, his breath
frosting up in the cold night air. He used to love the cold, crisp Chicago
nights. Now they just chilled him to his old bones, even only being out
in it for fifteen seconds or so.

"Good to hear," the young man carrying him said.

Both Saber and the young soldier knew that was all Saber could tell

13

him about the mission. Almost no one on Earth even knew about the *Earth Protection League.*

It was just safer that way.

The young soldier was a member of the *League,* of course, but unless he decided to spend twenty years on a slow shuttle that stayed under light speed, he'd never see anything beyond the moon until he got a lot older. So there was just no reason to tell him about the missions. The kid couldn't go out there. He was just too young to survive the age and time regression of the T-G flight.

The soldier carried Saber through the sliding door into his room and laid him gently in the bed.

Then the kid stepped back and saluted. "Great job, Captain. I'll see you again soon. Have a Merry Christmas."

"Thank you. You too."

The kid turned and then stopped, as if seeing a ghost.

It took Saber a moment to understand what the problem was. Then he saw Dot, the woman who lived across the hall, as she wheeled her chair out of the shadows of the corner.

Oh, no.

Saber didn't know what to think or even do. This was something he had never imagined happening.

Dot was his best friend here in the nursing home. He'd often wished he could tell her about his missions. But he was restricted from doing so by regulations.

The *EPL* had a lot of very firm regulations. Considering the nature of the job and who was doing the fighting, it had to be strict and clear.

The young soldier glanced back at him, a look of fear on his face, his hand on his gun on his hip.

Saber understood the reason for the kid's fear. If the case warranted, the young soldier was ordered to kill anyone who happened to get in the way of a mission.

Saber looked at his friend sitting there in her wheelchair clearly looking confused.

Dot wasn't in the way.

Tonight's mission was over.

"It's all right, soldier." Saber looked the young kid directly in the eyes and smiled. "She's a friend."

The young man stood for a moment, then nodded. "Understood, Captain. Command will be expecting a report on this."

"They will have it in the morning."

The young soldier nodded to Dot. "Goodnight, ma'am." He then vanished through the door, closing it behind him.

Saber lay on his back in his bed, his head turned, staring at Dot. He couldn't really see the expression on her face, and she said nothing.

He could feel his heart beating in his chest, and he hoped he still didn't smell like those aliens he had killed.

For the next few moments the silence in the room sounded like a roaring engine about to overwhelm them both, the ticking of his wall clock like the timer of a bomb.

Then finally Dot rolled a little closer to his bed and said, "Have I got you in some sort of trouble?"

Saber remembered the pitched fight he'd just had with six alien pirates, the success they had had again in defending the *Earth Protection League* and its space.

And the death of Sarah.

That was trouble.

Not this.

He laughed.

But he realized he was back in his old body and the laugh turned into a hacking, coughing, old man's laugh that lasted for a good thirty ticks of his clock before he finally stopped.

"You want to know where I was?" he asked.

She nodded.

He motioned her closer to his bed.

"You won't believe me, but I would love to tell you."

"You never know what I might believe," she said.

He laughed softly this time, avoiding the hacking cough.

"It's going to feel good to finally be able to tell you about my missions."

She nodded.

He couldn't believe it. After all the years of going out and coming back, of defending Earth against all odds, and all alien scum, he *finally* got to tell someone.

And for the next hour it felt wonderful.

Almost as good as killing those alien pirates.

Almost.

FOUR

DOT WAS MORE stunned than anything else.

Brian's wild story of being a Captain in the *Earth Protection League*, of fighting alien pirates in deep space as a young man, was outrageous to say the least.

He told her about how he had had to board a pirate ship, fight all six of them, and how bad they smelled. The details of the story were very clear, right down to how he kicked one of the dead bodies before he left the pirate ship.

She couldn't believe any of it, yet she had seen him be carried in and out of the room by a man who had called him Captain. And who wore a gun and was upset that she was there.

More than likely it was all just some wild fantasy Brian had paid a kid to help him carry out as a Christmas present to himself. After all, he'd only been gone from the room for twenty minutes, not three days like he had claimed.

Yet a part of her had wanted to believe his wild dream.

Especially the part about growing young again, because of how time and space and matter worked.

His explanation of that had almost been funny enough to laugh at. Yet when he had tried to explain it to her, she hadn't laughed. Just listened, hoping to not break the fantasy world he lived in.

She liked him enough to do that for him.

Especially on Christmas Eve.

It wasn't until the end of his wild story, after telling her about the loss of his crewmate, Sarah, that he asked her something that bothered her on a deep level. He asked if she was interested in joining up, being a soldier in the *Earth Protection League*, of being young again to help Earth fight whatever threatened its space borders.

The question bothered her a great deal, but instead of saying so, she laughed and said, "Who wouldn't like to be young again?"

"Great," he said. "I can't promise anything, but it never hurts to ask the brass in charge of it all."

At that moment, Joyce, the night nurse tonight, poked her head in and smiled at them. She asked if Brian needed anything, then winked at Dot and left.

Dot laughed and suddenly realized she hadn't yet made it to the bathroom.

"I'll see you at breakfast," she told Brian, heading for the door as fast as she could move her chair.

"Can't say anything about this to anyone," Brian said behind her.

Again she laughed as she went into the hall.

"Who would believe me?"

She didn't believe it.

Not one word of it.

But she wanted to.

FIVE

December 24th, 2018
Actual Earth Time
Location: Chicago

AT BREAKFAST ON Christmas Eve day, Brian was all smiles, his wheelchair pulled up to a table in the corner of the festively decorated lunchroom. No one else was sitting at the table.

Green and red garland hung from just about everything that wasn't needed, and the room smelled of a combination of Christmas wreathes and pancakes. Actually a pretty good smell as far as Dot was concerned.

Beyond the window, the Chicago weather had turned cold and clear, the sun almost too bright off the white ground. All the snow was going to freeze solid by the time the day was done and it got dark. It was lucky she wasn't going anywhere for Christmas tomorrow. The roads would be awful.

After all the years of living in this area, she knew that without a doubt. But she had no reason left in her life at this point to even step outside.

She had forced herself to do a little walking this morning, even though she was tired from being up so late and talking with Brian last night, so she moved along behind her wheelchair, slowing pushing it around the other tables so she could join him.

"Good morning," she said, sitting with her back to the window so she wouldn't be blinded from the bright sunlight. "Going to get cold tonight out there."

He glanced at the window behind her, then back at her, his smile growing even bigger. "I hadn't honestly noticed. But might be a problem for my son getting here later on."

She knew Brian had a son in the area, but hadn't met him in all the years they had known each other. Maybe today she would get a chance.

Brian waited for the orderly to give her some orange juice, ask if she would like her normal eggs and pancakes, and leave.

Then he leaned over slightly and whispered, "There's a mission tonight and League Command said that if I was willing to train you on the ship's proton weapons, you could join up. You would take Sarah's place. You'd be a private, but there's room for advancement."

"You're kidding, right?" Dot asked, staring at him.

He had shaved this morning, but his skin was still rough with light stubble, and there was a twinkle in his eye that she'd never seen before. "Not in the slightest," he said.

Then his expression got very serious and a coldness came into his eyes.

That made her sit back, surprised.

"But it's dangerous." His voice was a low whisper. "I won't kid you on that. You die out there and they bring your body back here and you're found dead in your sleep in the morning. The time travel part of things just doesn't revive anyone."

She hadn't been so confused in years. She took her red cloth napkin with some Christmas scene on it and unfolded it and put it on her lap to give her a moment to think.

Brian was seriously asking her to join in his delusions.

And he was telling her it was dangerous.

What were he and that friend that had carried him out going to do? Would Brian kill her if she went with them in the middle of the night?

Brian reached across and touched her hand.

She could feel the roughness of his hand against her brittle skin. It was the first time a man, other than an aide, had touched her in any way since her husband had died all those years ago.

"You said you wanted to be young again," he said, staring into her eyes with those intense brown eyes of his.

"I do," she said, moving her hand away.

"But you don't trust me, do you?" Brian said, smiling. The boyish twinkle was back in his eyes.

"Would you?" she asked. "You have to admit, your story is pretty wild stuff."

"I didn't believe it either, my first night," he said, laughing and clearly remembering something since he seemed to be looking off into the distance. After a moment he went on. "To be honest with you, even after going on more than a hundred missions, I still don't believe it."

"So I should just *trust you?*" she asked.

"How old are you, Dot?" he asked in return.

"Eighty-four," she said, squaring her shoulders. No man had asked her that question in years. She wasn't sure she liked telling a man her age. She was still very old-fashioned that way.

"I'm eighty-five," he said. "And this old body is getting worse by the day it seems. What I do for the *League* is a dream come true. At our age, what else do we have to live for but dreams?"

At that moment, for some crazy reason, she decided he was right. Maybe it was because it was Christmas Eve and there was a faint Christmas song playing in the background and the sun was shining and she would have no family visiting today.

Or just maybe she really didn't have anything to lose.

Either way she'd play along with him and his wild fantasy, maybe even let herself believe that she might be young again for a short time.

Every night she dreamed of dancing anyway. Why not join Brian in his dreams for a night?

"I'll go," she said, smiling at him.

The light in his eyes was like a child seeing the presents under a Christmas tree. She knew she had made the right decision.

With that the orderly brought their breakfast and they talked about family and Christmas memories.

And at lunch they sat together and did the same, sharing the past with each other. Dot learned more about Brian that day than she had in years. It seemed that because she was willing to go with him, he felt more open with her.

And she felt more open with him for some reason.

She really had made the right decision, she knew that.

She went to bed at her normal time of eight and managed to doze, but awoke at midnight, worried that she had made a really stupid decision.

She could hear Brian's clock ticking and not much else. The worry about what was going to happen kept her awake far too long and she kept waking up at any sound.

At one point she almost wheeled across the hall and told Brian to forget about her going along, but before she could get up enough energy to do that, she had just gone back to sleep, deciding she would deal with it in the morning.

It was three in the morning, Christmas morning, when the young woman dressed in black came across the hall from Brian's room.

Dot heard her coming because Brian had laughed.

Dot was suddenly scared out of her wits.

But the fact that there was a young woman also involved calmed her a little. It wasn't just Brian and some friend of his.

"My name is Lieutenant Sherri," the woman said, stopping beside her bed and smiling. "Brian says you're thinking of joining the League, Mrs. Leeds. I sure envy you."

Those words rocked Dot completely out of her fear, which drained away like someone had pulled a plug in a sink.

She looked up into the young dark eyes and the smiling face of Lieutenant Sherri over her bed. "Envy me? Why?"

"Because you get to go out there, into space, to defend Earth. It will be years before I can go, even on a short-run mission."

Dot only nodded.

She had no idea what the young woman had said or meant. And she still didn't believe she was going into space, but at this point she really didn't know what to believe was going to happen. But at least the fear was gone.

"Are you ready?" the young woman asked as she moved in beside Dot's bed and lowered the railing.

"Why not?" Dot said. "After all, it's Christmas morning."

The woman picked her up as easily as the orderly, stepped to the door and glanced down the hall to make sure the nurse wasn't watching. Then quickly, she carried Dot across the hall and into Brian's room.

Brian was already gone and the young woman carrying her didn't hesitate. She went right through Brian's open sliding glass door and out into the cold night air, her feet crunching on the frozen snow, her arms holding Dot gently, but firmly.

"Aren't I going to be missed?" Dot asked as the night air bit at her, sharp, pin-like. Not in a million years had she expected to go out into this cold night air.

"You'll be back in twenty minutes," the young woman said. "Everything is taken care of on this end."

"We won't be outside that long, will we?" Dot asked, starting to shiver. The older she had gotten, the more sensitive she had become to the cold. This was like a knife cutting at her skin.

"Only a moment," Lieutenant Sherri said.

The rest went like a blur for Dot.

One moment they were in the cold, then she and the woman carrying her were floating up through the air into something big above her in the night sky. That was a nightmare and Dot wanted to close her eyes, but didn't.

The minute they lifted off the ground, she started to really believe Brian's story.

And suddenly she was scared again.

The young Lieutenant Sherri walked her quickly down a hallway that looked like it could be a hallway on a cruise liner. Then she carried Dot into a single room.

The coffin-like sleep chamber in the small room was exactly like Brian had described.

Lieutenant Sherri laid her in the deep chamber, on the soft padding, and then pointed to a closet. "Your uniform is in there, made to fit you exactly. When you wake up, just shove the lid open and get dressed."

"How will I get out of this?" Dot asked, indicating the sleep chamber. She knew without a doubt she was too weak to push herself over the edge of something this deep.

The young lieutenant just laughed softly and then said with a smile, "Just trust me, you won't have any trouble."

With that the lieutenant closed the lid.

Before Dot could even think another thought or begin to panic, she was asleep.

SIX

December 25th, 1958
Equivalent Earth Time
Location: Deep Space

DOT DIDN'T DREAM, or at least she didn't remember dreaming.

She awoke without opening her eyes.

She was almost afraid to.

She could feel the softness of the padding under her, so she knew she wasn't in her own bed in the nursing home.

She could remember clearly the frightening moments of floating through the air above the Shady Valley Nursing Home and seeing the Chicago skyline out over the cold, clear winter's night.

Slowly, she opened her eyes to see the top of the lid of the sleep chamber. There was a faint light coming from around the edge and the top seemed much farther away than it actually was, more than likely to keep down claustrophobia.

She raised a hand and pushed the lid open, then stared at the skin on her bare arm.

Young skin.

Perfect skin, not the blemished, dried skin of an eighty-four year old woman.

Was that even possible?

Then she moved her leg.

It was as if her heart stopped at that moment.

Her breath caught and she wasn't sure if she was going to burst into tears.

Not since the accident that had killed her husband and crippled her had she been able to move her legs without a lot of work after waking up.

Yet now she could.

Both of them.

Easily.

She sat up and watched her legs move under her old nightgown.

Not possible, but she needed to really test this.

Quickly, not allowing herself to think about it, she swung herself up and out of the sleep chamber, landing on the floor, *on her feet*, as if she'd done that every day for years.

Now she really did feel like crying.

For a moment she just stood there shaking.

Brian had been telling the truth.

Or this really was the most vivid dream she had ever had.

She touched her own soft skin on her arms. It didn't feel like she was dreaming.

She glanced around.

She was alone in what looked to be a small cabin of a ship, the only furniture a bolted down chair and the coffin-like sleep chamber. This was the same room the woman had carried her into.

Dot quickly pulled off her nightgown and studied herself in a full-length mirror that was bolted to the back of the closet door.

It was her young body, all right. From her eighty-four year old mind, it looked perfect, even though she knew that in her twenties, she had thought her body far from perfect.

How little she had known then. She was one damn fine-looking broad, as they used to say.

That thought made her laugh. Her voice was higher and clearer to her ears than she remembered.

If she was going insane or this was some sort of trick, it was a great trick.

Then she opened the closet and started to get dressed.

As Lieutenant Sherri had said it would, the uniform fit perfectly.

How had anyone known her size when she was in her twenties?

The uniform consisted of undergarments that seemed very modern. White underwear and what seemed like a "sports bra" of some sort. She had never worn one, but she had heard of them. It felt far more comfortable than the old-fashioned things she wore most days.

There were brown leather pants, tall black boots, a silk blouse that fit loosely over the middle and tightly across her chest, and a leather vest with a triangle insignia on it that read *EPL*.

Earth Protection League.

So far everything Brian had told her was coming true.

How was any of this possible?

She studied herself in the mirror one more time. Never in her faintest memory did she look this good.

Finally, she turned and headed for the door, smiling, enjoying the feel of her feet solidly under her as she walked. The boots fit her feet perfectly, almost like a second skin.

It was time to see just exactly what this dream was all about before she woke up.

The door to her room slid open.

In the wide corridor on the other side two men stood, leaning against the wall. The corridor was painted a tan color with a rubber matting on the floor. Not like anything she had seen before.

One of the men was short, with light-brown hair and an infectious grin.

The other was a tall, square-shouldered, square jawed man with a handsome face and a thick head of wavy, brown hair.

They both looked to be in their early twenties and had on the same uniform as she did, only the tall, good-looking one had two weapons on his hips like an old gunslinger in the Wild West.

He pushed himself away from the wall with the ease of a man perfectly in touch with his body, then said, "Merry Christmas and welcome to my ship, *The Bad Business,* Private Dot Leeds. This is Lieutenant Carl Turner, my third in command."

Carl stuck out his hand, smiling. "Glad you decided to join us."

She nodded as she shook his hand, then glanced at the one who had introduced them.

She knew who he was, but for some reason her mind wasn't letting her admit it.

Was it really possible?

Finally, she asked, "Brian?"

He laughed, deep and rich and full of power. "Of course, but I'm afraid we have to be a little more formal on board ship. You need to call me Captain when we're on a mission like this."

She knew she was standing there, on her own two legs, her head shaking, completely stunned. More than likely her mouth was open, too.

Both men had the decency to not laugh out loud at her.

Captain Brian Saber smiled and touched her arm. His touch was almost shocking. Again, he was the only man except an orderly or nurse or doctor who had touched her in any way in decades.

"As I told you back at breakfast," Brian said, "I still think this is all a dream, too. But I'm afraid it's not."

His face got very serious and the cold, intense look she had seen in the nursing home was now in full force on this younger version. "You're going to get a quick dunk in the deep end with this mission, I'm afraid. We don't have much time."

"Why?" she managed to ask. "What do I need to do?"

"I've got to get back to the command center," Brian said. "Carl will get you checked out on the Photon Projector Beam weapons and what the enemy ships look like, and how to destroy them."

"Enemy?" she asked.

Now she was suddenly afraid again. She had never fired a weapon before and she didn't know if she could ever do it, let alone kill something.

Brian touched her shoulder in a reassuring way and it did calm her down a little.

"Good luck and I'll see you after it's all over."

With that, he turned and strode down the corridor, a man completely in charge of his world.

She watched him walk away. She had no idea that Brian had such force inside of him. At the age of eighty-five, such force was often hidden, or pounded out of a person.

She wondered how people saw her at eighty-four.

She took a deep breath, forcing herself to calm down, and turned to Carl's smiling face. "Well, show me what to do and how to do it and I'll see if I can carry my weight."

He laughed. "The Captain said you'd be a good addition to the crew. I think he just might be right."

"He did, huh?" she asked, glancing back in the direction that Captain Brian Saber had gone, as Carl led her off in the opposite direction. "Nice to know."

Then all the way down the corridor, she rejoiced in the feeling of actually walking without support again.

At one point she almost started skipping but managed to restrain herself.

Dream or no dream, simply walking again was the best Christmas present she could have ever asked for.

SEVEN

December 25th, 1958
Equivalent Earth Time
Location: Deep Space

THE COMMAND CENTER of *The Bad Business* was a picture of efficiency of design. Brian occupied the big center chair facing a wall of screens, controls and computer pads covering both arms of the big chair. He was the pilot and he could make his ship almost dance from that chair.

The Command Center was actually fairly small, with only four stations. Marian Knudson, a stunning redhead from Wisconsin, sat in the chair to his left, tucked up under a wide board of control panels and display screens. She did everything, often a half second of when Brian needed it, as if she could read his mind.

In the chair to his right was Carl Turner, the best navigator in the fleet. And one of the smartest people Brian had ever met.

Brian loved this small command center more than any place he had ever been in his entire life. It was the brains and heart of a very powerful warship, sitting in the top of the head of the bird-shaped ship. He liked the electronics smell, the sounds of faint alarms as systems went through checklists, and he really loved the feel of the thick, leather chair that perfectly fit his young form.

But at this moment, all three of them were moving as fast as they could as he took his ship through and at the enemy as hard and as fast as *The Bad Business* would go.

The Astra Warsticks were long, thin things that resembled a straw with something stuck in both ends more than a spaceship. At full length, they were about the same length as his ship, and very deadly.

He dove in again at one of them, twisting to give his gunners open shots, then quickly used evasive maneuvers to avoid getting hit by the Warstick Slicing Energy Beam weapons that shot from each end of their ships like orange fluid blown out of a drinking straw.

He was trying to do everything in his power to make this a fight, but he doubted it would last long.

"Damn," Carl muttered under his breath on Saber's right as Saber barely avoided flying directly into one of the energy beams from a Warstick.

Damn was right. That had been too close. He swung the ship out wide and made a pass along the length of a turning Warstick, letting his gunners hammer at it.

Commander Marian Knudson, his second in command, sat silently on his left, her red hair pulled back off her face, her fingers dancing over the control board, making sure that he had all the information and was in contact with all the other ships at any moment, knowing where they all were.

The three of them, the only three in the control room, worked like a single person. They had done over twenty missions together and really liked each other.

But little good that was going to do them today.

Brian knew that no one at *Earth Protection League* Command

thought he, or the other twenty *EPL* ships sent to this battle, would survive.

The Astra had decided to take six *League* systems. They had given Earth ten hours to turn them over, and when Earth had said no, the Astra had sent two hundred Warsticks across the border.

Saber and the other *EPL* ship's job was simply to slow the Astra down while the *League* mounted a better, and more powerful defense closer to the threatened systems.

Saber guessed the *League* figured that twenty ships full of old, nursing home residents were expendable when it came to defending Earth's space.

And Saber agreed.

He and the rest *were* expendable when it came down to fighting off the alien scum and protecting Earth and its allies.

But Brian didn't plan on getting killed or even beaten up just yet, especially by an alien that looked more like a piece of straw than an alien warrior.

But at the moment, that was exactly what was happening. From Marian's report, the *EPL* ships had managed to destroy six of the Warsticks, but had lost three of their ships in the process.

They were going to slow the Warstick fleet down, that was for sure, but they weren't going to stop it by a long ways, unless he came up with something fast.

Suddenly the voice of Dot came over the ship's communications link. "Captain?"

"Go ahead, Private," he said.

His stomach twisted and he felt sick. In the battle he had forgotten she was even on board. What a mission to be her first. And most likely her last. If they were killed, Shady Valley Nursing Home would have two deaths in one Christmas morning.

"Our weapons are doing no good against the sides of these ships," Dot said. "But I have an idea that is pretty far-fetched."

"Anything at this point," he said, moving the ship barely out of the way of two closing Warsticks trying to trap him between their open ends.

"From what the Lieutenant told me," she said, "the Warstick control room is near one end, their engine room is near the other, and weapons are fired from both ends."

"Got it right," Saber said. "What's your idea?"

"I think if you cut one of those sticks in half," she said, "you might put it out of business."

"And how would you suggest we do that?" Saber asked. Then almost before the question was out of his mouth, he knew the answer.

"Ram it," he said.

At the same moment she said, "Ram it."

"Great idea, Private," he said, suddenly feeling like they just might have a chance. A slim chance on a crazy idea, but it just might work.

He went to ship-wide com. "I want all weapons aimed forward and firing. On my mark."

The Warsticks were very thin right at the center, so the Earth ships had a complete advantage in size. And the Earth ships had great forward screens since they flew so fast through space with the Trans-Galactic drive.

In fact, at full T-G drive speed, the ship could punch a hole through a small moon and come out the other side. But this close they wouldn't be able to get to full speed or full screens that only came up at higher speeds.

He swung the ship around and headed for the center of the nearest Warstick.

One problem the sticks had was turning quickly and he stayed easily ahead of the Warstick's evasive turn.

"Asteroid deflectors and shields on full!" Brian ordered.

"Already on," Carl said.

"Brace for impact!" Marian announced to the entire crew.

It was almost anticlimactic.

The ship didn't even bump. Saber had felt a worse impact running over a jackrabbit with a car back in Idaho when he was younger.

But the Warstick was cut in half. The two halves spinning away from the collision point.

A moment later, both ends of the enemy Warstick exploded in bright white flashes.

"Well, I'd say that worked," Carl said, looking over and smiling at Brian.

"I'll be a blonde," Marian said, her favorite phrase of surprise. Considering her bright red hair, that just wasn't ever possible, which is why the statement worked.

"Inform the other ships," Brian ordered. "Weapons crew, keep firing forward. Let's take out another one."

He swung the ship around and plowed through the center of another Warstick before it could even begin to turn out of his way.

The same thing happened.

They went through the alien ship as if it wasn't even there, then separated halves of the Warstick exploded.

Maybe, just maybe, they had a chance in this fight. For the first time in a few hours, he was starting to hope he might see one more Christmas turkey dinner at the nursing home.

And with luck he would see Dot again. If they survived this, he had a surprise for her that he had been thinking about long before he invited her to join the *League*.

Two hours of hard fighting later, the Astra Warstick fleet, or what was left of it, turned and headed back for the border. There were still fifteen of the twenty Earth Protection League ships left.

They had won and won easily.

Brian reported to League Command what had happened, then sat back in his chair and took a long, deep breath. He had been sweating for hours and could desperately use a shower. He could feel himself sticking to his shirt and his chair.

But he hadn't felt this good about a mission in a long, long time.

"Nice flying, Captain," Carl said, also slouching in his chair, clearly as exhausted as Brian felt. But he had a huge smile on his tired face.

"That was almost fun," Marian said, sighing as well. "Let's not do it again for a few years, okay?"

"Agreed," Brian said, thinking about how Dot must be feeling right now. "I think this deserves a party, don't you?"

"I think the fact that we're still alive deserves something," Carl said, laughing.

"I will even drink to that," Marian said.

"Oh, God," Carl said, "a drunk redhead. That's what we need."

"Exactly what the Captain ordered," Brian said, laughing along with his two command crew.

Saber flicked the communication switch to the members of his crew. "Congratulations people, on a job well done. And special thanks to our newest crew member, Private Dot Leeds. Party in one hour, everyone. Don't be late."

EIGHT

December 25th, 1958
Equivalent Earth Time
Location: Deep Space

DOT SMILED AT the Captain's words and for the first time in two hours let go of the control stick for the Proton Projector Beam weapon, then sat back in her padded chair.

She couldn't remember the last time she had felt so tired and so exhilarated at the same time.

The battle had seemed to go on forever. Flashing ship after flashing ship, at times she didn't know what to fire at and when. But she didn't think she fired at any *EPL* ships.

They were pretty amazing-looking, designed like big birds and she now knew Brian and Carl were in the command area in what looked like the top of the head.

At first she didn't think she could fire a weapon, but then she started to learn quickly when she saw the alien ships that looked like thin hourglasses. She had broken an hourglass timer once when

36

cooking back when she was married and that's what had given her the idea to break the two ends in half.

From there the battle seemed like it had just started and then it ended.

Behind her, Private Becky Pollard came up and patted her on the back. Becky was a stout woman with a bright smile. She had been the gunner behind Dot and to the right.

"Nice job. Much better than my first time out here."

"Thanks," Dot said, standing and stretching muscles that back in the nursing home she could barely move.

Becky was shorter than Dot's five-four, with blonde hair and freckles. During the battle she swore more than any person Dot had ever heard, using words Dot had never dreamed a woman could use so effectively.

"I had no idea what I was doing," Dot said.

"How could you?" Becky asked, laughing with a throaty sound that seemed to be both natural and from too many cigarettes. "Remember where you were when the Captain asked you to join the crew."

"A nursing home wheelchair," Dot said, smiling and shaking her head as the memories flooding back in.

And the questions came back as well about this all being a dream. It didn't feel much like a dream anymore, that was for sure.

"Being in a nursing home sure trains you to fire a Proton Projector Beam weapon, doesn't it?" Becky said.

"I wish I had one for a few of the day nurses," Dot said.

Becky snorted and then laughed again. "Yeah, I know that feeling. Come on, I'll show you where a shower is, and you should have another fresh uniform in your room."

"Thanks," Dot said. Then, almost as if it had been a habit for the past twenty-five years, she took the first step.

And then she remembered that before this trip, she couldn't walk well and without work. And hadn't been able to for over twenty-five years.

This was a dream.

It had to be.

One hour later, freshly showered and still marveling at her ability to walk like a young person, she joined the rest of the crew in the mess area.

The place was about the twice the size of a large living room and smelled of fresh bread. It was larger by about half than the lunchroom at Shady Valley Nursing Home.

All the tables had been pushed against the walls leaving the smooth floor open in the middle. The crew of about forty or so milled around the outside, smiling and laughing.

She couldn't believe it. All of those young people around here were really old people back on Earth.

Drinks and food filled one table near the door, and she took a bottle of water and some fresh bread.

Becky came over and introduced her to about ten of the crew members who all seemed pleased to meet her. When they gave their names, they also gave their town. She liked that.

Finally she moved over to Captain Brian Saber who was talking with a redhead that someone said was Commander Marian Knudson, his second in command.

"Thanks for the great idea of ramming the Warsticks," he said, taking her bottle of water and handing her a drink that looked like a cross between a screwdriver and something with red juice in it. "You saved all of our lives."

She laughed. "You'd have thought of it eventually."

"Maybe, maybe not," he said. "No one in any battle with the Warsticks has ever thought of it in years. So thanks."

"You're welcome."

She knew her face was red, but she ignored the feeling and sipped at the drink, loving the sweet flavor mixed with the orange juice.

She couldn't believe she was standing, talking with Brian, on a ship that looked like a big bird, after a battle with aliens. Now she understood why she hadn't believed him when he told her about his last mission.

She didn't believe she was here, to be honest.

The Captain turned to Carl who looked like he was drinking straight scotch and said, "Fire it up."

"You got it, Captain," Carl said, smiling at her before moving away.

Carl tapped a button on a wall and music filled the room.

Christmas music, just soft enough to talk over, yet loud enough to hear clearly.

The song was an old Benny Goodman Christmas song she couldn't remember the title to, but she had loved to dance to it back when she was young. It had been an old song then, but she hadn't cared.

The Captain bowed to her slightly. "I remember in one of our lunch conversations you mentioned how much you liked to dance. And you mentioned this song. So I figured what better thing to do on Christmas than dance?"

For a moment she was sure she would wake up and lose the entire dream.

But she didn't.

She stayed right there, standing on her own two feet.

The music swirled around her, the handsome man smiled at her, the room felt perfect.

"I'd love to," she managed to say to the Captain.

She handed her drink to Marian who smiled and nodded to her.

Captain Brian Saber, the most handsome man she could ever remember seeing, took her hand and stepped to the middle of the open floor.

A moment later they were moving around the floor of the mess hall as the other crew members watched and clapped along with the music.

She was dreaming.

And it was wonderful.

And she didn't care.

All she focused on was his firm grasp, his strong muscles under his silk shirt, and his twinkling eyes and infectious smile.

She could do this all night.

Four hours later, after more dances than she could remember, she was standing beside the coffin-like sleep chamber again in the cabin they had assigned her.

She had put on the old nightgown over her young body. She knew she had to get in the chamber, but she didn't want to.

She stood there, swaying back and forth, trying to get the memory of the dancing, of just standing, clearly in her mind.

And the memory of being held by Captain Brian Saber.

She really, really needed to remember this dream.

Finally, when the warning bell rang, she had no choice.

With one last twirl on her feet, she crawled in and pulled the cover closed over her head.

The next thing she remembered, Lieutenant Sherri, dressed in black, was picking her up out of the sleep chamber and taking her down into the courtyard, floating in the cold Chicago night air.

A few minutes later, the lieutenant put her down in her wheelchair, saluted, and left.

Dot looked at her old, wrinkled hands in the dim light, then felt the deadness in her legs.

Had she been dancing on those legs?

Had it really happened?

Had she just dreamed it all?

It had been a wonderful dream. The battle had been scary, but the dancing and being young had been more than she could have ever imagined.

She needed to try to find out the answer to those questions.

She moved her chair out across the hall and through Brian's door.

He was in bed, his head turned so that he could see her as she rolled up beside him.

Even in the dim light, she could see his smile and the twinkle in his eyes.

"You've got a lot of explaining to do," she said, "before I'm really going to believe that all happened."

He laughed, managing to not cough. "I felt exactly the same way at first. And every time I end up back here in this old worthless body, I wonder if I actually did everything I remember doing."

"So it was real?" she asked, looking around the nursing home room, so far from the ship on the edge of the borders between Earth's space and other alien races. The room was in a faint light from the hall and the nightlight in the bathroom. The big wall clock ticked, filling the room with a constant reminder that time was moving forward.

This was so far from the battle with the Warsticks.

"Very real," Brian said. "And very important. We're the only ones that can go out there and defend this planet. We're the only ones old enough to withstand the time travel length to get to the edges of the *EPL* borders."

He paused for a moment and the clock ticking got seemingly even louder.

Then he said firmly, "Earth needs us. Amazing as that may seem."

A shiver ran down her back and she took a deep breath, looking into the wonderful eyes of Brian Saber.

"I thought I was long past the point where anyone would ever need me."

"A few years ago," Brian said, "so did I."

They sat in silence for a moment, letting the clock tick on.

Finally she took a deep breath and realized just how tired she felt.

She slowly pushed her wheelchair back from his bed and turned it toward the door.

"Join me for Christmas breakfast?" she asked.

"I'd love to," he said, smiling. "And maybe soon we can go dancing again."

"Do you think that's possible? Really?"

"We're usually called for a mission at least once a week, if not more often," he said. "I think a dance or two just might be arranged."

"Thank you, Captain," she said. "For the best Christmas present anyone has ever given me. I will see you at breakfast."

"The pleasure will be all mine," he said.

She wheeled herself across the hall and to her bed.

A few moments later she was on her back, staring at the ceiling, remembering the feeling of standing, of walking without help, and of dancing.

Especially dancing.

She so loved to dance.

Tonight hadn't been a dream. She knew that now. She had fought aliens for the *Earth Protection League*.

She had danced with the most handsome man she had ever met.

And she would dance again.

For the first time in years, she actually had something to live for. Tomorrow at breakfast, she'd talk to Captain Brian Saber about all the wonders out there in the universe.

About her duties.

And what Earth needed from her.

It felt wonderful to be needed again, especially on Christmas.

She closed her eyes after a few minutes and drifted off to sleep.

And for the first night in a very long time, she didn't need to dream of dancing.

PART TWO
THE SECOND MAJOR MISSION

OVER TWO YEARS LATER

NINE

February 12th, 2021
Actual Earth Time
Location: Chicago

DOT WAS FEEDING Brian his applesauce one spoonful at a time when he saw their target.

Around them, the Shady Valley Nursing Home went on with its normal lunch routine, but today was going to be anything but normal. In fact, the survival of the human race might depend on what happened next.

He didn't want to think about the cost of failure. As the cliché often said, failure was not an option this time around.

The banging of dishes and the rumble of people talking made it almost impossible for Brian to be heard. So he and Dot had a signal for when he wanted her to stop with her feeding him his applesauce, about the only solid thing he could really eat these days. He didn't much mind, since the stroke had also taken his ability to taste anything.

And smell anything, and considering how little control he had of certain body functions since the stroke, he considered that a gift.

He blinked his right eye and she instantly pulled back, taking a napkin and wiping the drool from his chin.

Being eighty-eight was bad enough, but being mostly paralyzed from a series of strokes really sucked more than Brian could ever say. Thankfully Dorothy "Dot" Leeds made it bearable. And took care of him far more than she should. But she said she loved doing it and didn't mind in the slightest.

She was his best friend and had been for years before she had joined the *Earth Protection League*. Now they were in love, but both of them were slowly dancing around that topic.

The last stroke he had a year ago had taken most of his movement, but not his mind, and he could still speak, mostly softly.

He blinked twice, their signal for Dot to get close. She leaned in so she could hear his hoarse whisper over the noise of the others eating lunch, her wonderful, eighty-seven-year-old face still showing the signs of the beautiful younger woman he knew so well.

"What is it, Brian?" she asked.

She then turned her ear slightly so she could hear him clearly over the noise. They had had many great conversations in that very fashion.

"Doctor Jack Dalton, sitting at the second table over."

Her head snapped around to find Dalton.

Then she turned back to Brian, her eyes bright. "Heavy, brown, knitted sweater with the orange food stains?"

"Yes," Brian whispered.

He wished he could have nodded, but that wasn't possible anymore.

They both watched for a moment while Dalton struggled with a plate of food on a tray before he managed to get it arranged. His hands were twisted almost closed by years of arthritis, and they shook.

Brian had no idea how Dalton could even hold a spoon, but somehow he managed, which was a lot better than Brian could do.

Dalton's very thin gray hair didn't do anything to cover a mottled scalp, and his thick, gray eyebrows seemed more like large bugs on his wrinkled face than anything else.

That man, that ninety-one-year-old scientist, had to be on the mission with them in the next few hours. Or Earth and the entire *Earth Protection League* might not survive. That's what the generals had told them this morning.

Dot and Brian had been given the responsibility of recruiting Dalton. Brian had no idea how they were going to do that. Not a clue, short of just kidnapping him, with help from younger *EPL* service people, of course. He doubted he and Dot combined could kidnap a plate of food from the lunchroom without help and planning.

Brian knew that likely the mission would be a suicide mission. If Dr. Jack Dalton did come with them, there would be a high chance he would never return to Shady Valley Nursing Home.

Of course, if he didn't come and didn't help, there was a high chance that none of them would return.

And that Earth and Shady Valley Nursing Home might not even survive.

As Brian had always figured, it was better to die out in space fighting than sitting in a wheelchair with drool on his chin.

This mission would be no exception to that.

TEN

February 12th, 2021
Actual Earth Time
Location: Chicago

AFTER SEEING DALTON, Brian wasn't hungry, but Dot insisted on finishing feeding him, whispering to him that he had to have his strength up for the sex later on.

That made him blush. She liked when she could get the great Captain Brian Saber to blush.

Then she finished her lunch as well, and with some help from an orderly got Brian's wheelchair moved out into the hall where they could intercept Dalton when he came out of the lunchroom.

She could walk along behind his chair pushing it slowly, but getting him out of that cluster of tables and chairs of the lunchroom was always too much for her.

She stood, holding onto the back of Brian's chair, thinking and waiting.

This was so important, she had no idea how they were going to make it happen, and she was scared, more scared than she had been piloting any ship over the last few years.

They had to make this happen. They had no choice from what the general had told her in a rage call direct to her phone this morning. Never before had she been contacted by anyone from the *EPL* directly in her room.

Brian said that had only happened to him once as well, and they had almost lost Earth in that battle.

Brian's finger tapped the arm of his wheelchair and she looked up.

Dalton was using a cane as he slowly approached, his hand knotted around the top of the cane.

She stepped forward, holding onto Brian's chair but standing beside it.

"Doctor, my name is Dot Leeds and this is Brian Saber. Could we have a minute to talk to you?"

Dot had left off their Captain titles purposefully. She had become a captain of her own ship just over a year ago. She had made it to captain faster than even Brian had. But she had had Brian helping her.

Now, with Dalton, there was simply no point in making the guy think they were crazy right off. He was going to think that anyway in a few minutes as it was.

She remembered she thought Brian was crazy when he told her about the *Earth Protection League*.

"I'm not a medical doctor," Dalton said, slowly moving to go past them.

"I know that, Doctor Dalton," Dot said. "Until you wrote a paper on the subatomic connection between space and time and matter, you were considered one of the top physicists of all time. Maybe greater than Einstein."

That stopped him, so Dot kept going.

"Please, just a few minutes of your time?" Dot asked. "I know you are new here, just arrived last week, but there is something urgent we need to talk to you about."

She could tell that Brian wanted to give her some support, but the best he could do was a slight nod and even that was amazing. That stroke had taken so much from him a year ago.

Thankfully, what happened to this body here on Earth didn't affect him at all sixty years out in space.

Dalton stared at her for a moment, then at Brian. Finally, he nodded. "I guess I don't have much else to do."

Step one down. Dot could feel the relief.

Now came the hard part.

As Dot moved around behind Brian to push him behind Dalton, she noticed Brian managed to slide one finger over the edge of his chair and push a hidden button on his wheelchair signaling the *League* to stand ready.

Good. At least that much was done.

"In here," Dalton said, moving toward his room as they had figured he would do. He had a private room, as they all did. The *League* could be in his room within seconds when Dot gave Brian the signal to push the button again.

And Dalton's room had a somewhat sheltered sliding door to the interior garden, lawn, and patio area that the home surrounded. That would be the way they would all leave.

She knew for a fact she wouldn't be going back to her room today for her normal after-lunch nap. Both she and Brian would be doing a rare daytime extraction for this mission.

That's how important it was.

And if they didn't win this coming battle, she wouldn't be seeing her room ever again either.

Doctor Dalton went into his room and pulled a chair over, then got another one for Dot.

The room looked the same as the rest of the rooms, but Dalton had an old table surrounded by three chairs. He had some papers on the table and had clearly been working on something there.

Dot wheeled Brian to a position between the chairs, then using the bar on the end of Dalton's bed, she went back and closed the door, lowering the room into almost complete silence.

"So what's this all about?" Dalton asked. "And what could be so important that you would need to talk urgently with someone as old and discredited as I am?"

"Eventually your name will be honored," Dot said, smiling at Dalton as she sat beside Brian. "Because your theories are completely right. But you won't live to see it, I'm afraid."

He laughed. "What? Are they sending old people back from the future?"

Brian cleared his throat and then said as loudly as he could, "That's not how your theory works, is it, Doctor?"

Dot was impressed that Brian could talk that loudly.

Dalton again laughed. "No, it isn't."

"You suggested in your work," Dot said, "that time and matter and space are connected. Completely connected — not in the way most scientists believe, but in much deeper ways, correct?"

"Yes, so what?"

"You happen to be the right age," Brian said, "to help out humanity with that wonderful mind of yours, and maybe save us all."

He just stared at Brian and shook his head.

"Doctor, please listen to me all the way through," Dot said. "I am certain you will not believe me, but when I tell this story, please keep in mind your very own theory. Please? The story will only take a few minutes."

"I suppose my nap can wait that long," he said, shrugging.

Dot smiled.

She indicated Brian. "This is Captain Brian Saber, the most decorated ship's captain in all of the *Earth Protection League*. My name is Captain Dorothy Leeds, but my friends call me Dot."

The Doctor started to speak, but Dot held up a hand to silence him. "The entire story first," she said.

"The *Earth Protection League* was formed back in a time long before Atlantis, when mankind first reached out into space. We were helped by other races we met in our local space neighborhood, and the *League* was formed and maintained even as mankind kept falling back into dark ages. Since governments don't last, no government knows about it."

"As years went by..." Brian said, his voice as clear as Dot had heard it in some time. Clearly he felt it critical that he help. He was always such a fighter. That was one of the many things she loved about him.

Brian took a deep breath and went on. "The *EPL* expanded its borders farther and farther out into space. The *EPL* now controls, with the help of many other races, a sphere sixty-plus light years around Earth."

"For centuries," Dot said, picking up the story, "everything was fine, until about ten years ago Earth-time. The *League* was suddenly attacked by what we call 'The Dogs,' an alien race bent on taking over and destroying Earth and all of Earth's allies."

Dalton started to say something, but Dot held up her hand and stopped him. Then she went on. "The Dogs were eventually beaten and pushed back to their borders, but not without a great loss of life on all the Earth bases out closer to the frontiers."

"So the *League* needed help," Brian said. "But because of your theory, it would be difficult to get help from Earth to the border quickly."

"They needed *old* help because of the very thing your theory described, Doctor," Dot said. "I don't really understand it, but it was explained to me that matter and time and space are permanently linked. So when a person climbs into a ship that can move through warped space, and thus get to a location great distances away quickly, the mass of the human body is still attached to its original space and time."

"In other words," Brian said, "I am eighty-eight sitting here. But if I go out sixty light-years using the Trans-Galactic Drive, I will arrive twenty-eight years old. And when I make the return voyage, arriving here within a half hour of when I leave, my body is again back to this state and age."

That amount of talking clearly tired Brian out. Dot could see that and she slipped his oxygen mask over his nose for a moment. He hated being in that old body. Just flat hated it. And she didn't blame him either.

"Over the centuries," Dot said, continuing the story that Dalton needed to hear, "scientists have managed to shelter the brain waves and thought patterns from the changes that happen as a body moves through great distances, so we keep our older minds in our younger bodies."

"You two are writing a book, aren't you? Some sort of science fiction book to make fun of my theories."

"We are not," Dot said, staring at Dalton. He was clearly angry and those bushy eyebrows were clutched together. "And they're *your* theories, Doctor. You proposed them; you had to know this would be an upshot of your theory if you were correct."

That shut the great physicist up completely.

The silence in the room seemed to crash in around them. Dot could hear her own heart beating and from what she could tell, Brian was breathing a little harder than normal.

Dalton leaned back, his old hands trembling, his face suddenly tired, but he was clearly thinking.

Finally, after a long moment of silence, he asked, "Why are you telling me this?"

"Because the *Earth Protection League* needs your help," Dot said. "Way beyond me to explain what they need you to do. Our job was to recruit you. And go with you. And have our ships run support for you."

"Into space?" Dalton asked.

"Into deep space," Dot said, nodding, keeping her intense gaze on the doctor. But as she did, she signaled to Brian with her right hand by pinching her fingers together.

It was time.

She could see out of the corner of her eye as Brian eased his finger toward the button that would call in the *League* to extract them. And then pushed it.

Dot took her gaze from Dalton and took off Brian's oxygen mask. In a moment he wouldn't need it.

"I'm not sure who is crazier," Dalton said, "you two, or me for listening to you."

"Isn't that what your critics said about you?" Brian asked, staring at the doctor. "Wouldn't you like to know, prove to yourself, that you were right?"

"You have no remaining family," Dot said, softly. "You are in this place until your last days. Alone. Trust me, going on missions is what Brian and I and our crews wait for, hold onto life for. Being young is wonderful. Being young with old, experienced minds, is even better. It makes living in a place like this worth the pain."

Dalton just sat there, saying nothing.

She and Brian had known that Dalton could never allow himself to agree. Just as both of them had never really said, "yes" to that first mission when they were recruited. It was just too crazy-sounding for any sane person to believe.

"We're going to prove this to you, Doctor," Brian said, as the sliding door leading out to the courtyard opened up and four young men and one woman walked in.

All were wearing civilian clothes, as was normal for extractions. But Dot knew all of them were Earth-bound members of the *EPL*. Or at least they would be Earth-bound until they got a lot older and could travel distances into space.

All five stopped and snapped off salutes to Brian and Dot.

Kennison, the young man who often carried Brian to the lift point, came over beside Brian, while the young woman named Sherri moved over beside Dot.

Dot stood.

She prided herself in walking to the extraction point, but it was always good to have an arm to hold onto.

The other three men flanked Doctor Dalton.

"It seems I have no choice but to play along with whatever this is," he said, standing slowly.

"You will believe us shortly," Dot said. "We'll talk again about sixty light-years from here."

With that Kennison picked Brian up like he didn't weigh anything.

Dot had to admit, the kid was gentle on Brian's old, thin skin, and Dot knew Brian appreciated that.

Kennison and Brian vanished just a step outside the door, leaving Doctor Dalton standing there, staring, with his mouth open. Usually, at night, they took them all the way to the center of the courtyard and used a tractor beam to lift them up. But it seemed, with a daylight extraction, the *League* was willing to take more chances.

"A form of teleportation," Dot said.

The doctor looked like he might have a heart attack before he got out of the room.

A moment later he and the three vanished just outside the door and then she let Sherri escort her out and pull the sliding door closed behind them before they were taken to the ship.

A moment later she was in the Trans-Galactic Drive transport ship in orbit and Sherri was lifting her and placing her gently into her sleep coffin.

Then she stepped back and snapped off a salute. "Have a safe voyage, Captain."

"Thanks," Dot said, giving a slight salute as the coffin lid closed over her.

She really, really hoped that she would see Sherri again. But that would only happen if she lived through the mission and they were successful.

And from what the general had hinted at on the phone this morning, that was doubtful.

ELEVEN

February 12th, 1961
Equivalent Earth Time
Location: Deep Space

BRIAN AWOKE AS usual to the faint, orange and rose smell of the sleep gas being flushed out of his sleep coffin. He reached up and pushed the lid open, relishing once again how wonderful it felt to actually be able to move his arms.

Move anything for that matter.

He sat up, and then levered himself out of the sleep coffin. He still had on his old clothes with the applesauce stains from breakfast, but he shed them quickly.

They did not smell good at all and he wrinkled his nose and tossed them into a cleaning bag to be washed while he was here. If he survived, the least he could do was have clean clothes going back.

He sometimes wondered how Dot put up with him in that old stroke-riddled body.

The room he awoke in wasn't his normal Captain's cabin on his

56

own ship, *The Bad Business*. This looked more like a normal stateroom on a transport ship. All his clothes and gear were on a small dresser.

They usually transferred their sleep coffins to their cabins before they awoke anyone. That meant Dot was here on the transport as well, instead of in her cabin in her ship, *The Blooming Rose*.

He guessed they were going to talk to the doctor here, before heading out on the mission.

Brian quickly slipped on the black leather pants and white, pleated, silk shirt that was the standard Captain's uniform. He put on the black leather vest with the *EPL* logo on the front over his shirt, then buckled on the wide black-leather belt around his waist.

He sat down and pulled on the soft leather boots, tucking his pants legs loosely into the top of the tall boots. Then he took his two photon-blasters from the top of the dresser and put them in their holsters on his belt.

Captain Saber was back.

He stood and just stared in the mirror for a moment, just as he did with every mission, trying to make himself believe this was real, that the young Saber was standing there, not the old, stroke-damaged Saber who lived on Earth and couldn't move.

He hoped at some point to ask Dot to marry him and file for permission to settle down on a planet out here on the frontier, maybe even have some kids and work on growing old once again, doing only local missions. That was his plan, but right now he and Dot were taking it slow. They both had previous spouses they both had loved. It felt odd to be starting over again at such an advanced age.

But he loved her. At some point he would get the courage to ask her to marry him. The rules were that you could only settle out here on the edge of the *EPL* if you were married, except for rare cases.

But right now, instead of thinking about marrying Dot, he had another mission to complete if he had any hope of ever having that happen.

He opened the stateroom door and headed down the hallway

toward the ship's lounge. That's where the crew would take the doctor when they woke him.

As he turned the corner, Brian saw Dot striding toward him, dressed as he was, but with only one Photon Blaster on her hip.

She was the most beautiful woman he had ever seen. Her wonderful brown hair was pulled back and her smile filled the corridor. She never once failed in taking his breath away.

"Hi, handsome," she said, kissing him firmly.

He kissed her back, not wanting to let her go.

Finally she laughed. "I told you that applesauce would get you going."

"Trust me," he said, "it's not the applesauce."

With that, they both laughed and turned and went into the lounge.

Doctor Dalton stood near the huge window that looked out over the fleet of ships surrounding the transport ship. From the number, it looked like the League was expecting all sorts of trouble on this mission.

The *EPL* ships looked more like a large flock of birds floating there in space than anything. Even to Brian they looked impressive.

Brian dismissed the guard standing beside the door and he and Dot moved over toward the doctor, through the tables and chairs that filled the lounge area around a small dance floor. He and Dot had spent many a fun evening in this lounge and on that dance floor before returning to Earth.

Dancing was something he loved to remember when trapped in that old body.

Dot loved it more than he did.

The doctor was standing with his left hand pressed flat against the window, staring around his hand at all the stars.

He looked just like a younger version of the man in the nursing home, only his hair was thick and his face much smoother. He still had the extremely thick eyebrows. And, of course, his hands were clearly healthy, something that seemed to be amazing him even more than the space and the fleet of ships.

He just kept pushing his hand flat against the view port, then looking at it.

"Doctor," Brian said. "I'm Captain Saber. This is Captain Leeds."

Dalton turned and looked at them, then just shook his head. "The two from the nursing home? How is that possible? How is any of this possible?"

"Yes, sir," Dot said. "It's possible because your theories are correct."

He stared at his hand as he opened and closed it.

He and Dot stood there silently, letting the great mind inside that head fight to grasp the evidence in front of him.

Then Dalton looked up at them. "I was right? I actually was right?"

"You were, sir," Brian said, nodding. "We are sixty light years from Earth. You are in your thirty-one-year-old body, the exact same body you had sixty years ago."

He pulled up the clean white shirt the service had supplied him and stared at the scar on his stomach. "Even my appendix is still gone. Lost that when I was twenty-seven."

"If we had gone four more light years out," Brian said, "you would still have it."

Dalton nodded, then turned again and put his hand on the window, pushing it flat, something he clearly couldn't do in his old body back on Earth.

After a moment, he turned back and looked at Brian. "Captain Saber, there was a reason you and Captain Leeds didn't let me live out my last days not knowing the truth. And I'm sure it was not simply a gesture of kindness. So what can I do for the *League*, as you call it, to earn my keep?"

Brian smiled, glad that the doctor had come around so quickly.

"I honestly don't know for sure," Brian said. "I will let the *League* scientists brief you. However I do know that our enemy, the Dogs, have somehow designed some sort of major weapon that has the chance of disconnecting time and space and matter."

He thought for a moment, finally shaking his head. "I can't imagine how that would be possible, now that I know my theory was correct. But I also don't understand how it could be used as a weapon."

Brian pointed at the fleet as Dot told him the answer.

"Almost all of the crews of all those battleships are senior citizens from Earth, just as the three of us are. It was the only choice the *League* had to get recruits quickly after we lost so many in that first war with the Dogs."

The doctor nodded. "Sever the connection, and we end up back on Earth, in our old bodies."

"And the frontier of the *Earth Protection League*," Brian said, "all the *League*, actually, will be undermanned and outgunned. All these warships would be suddenly empty. The *League* would fall."

Dalton nodded, giving one last look at the ships floating outside the big window.

"Where are the *Earth Protection League* scientists? I will need to get caught up quickly if I am to help."

Brian pointed at the largest ship in the center of the fleet. "They are on the admiral's ship, the *Tuesday Morning*.

"Can you take me there?" Dalton asked, again seeming to get lost in the fantastic view of ships and stars.

"You'll be taken there," Brian said. "Captain Leeds and I have our own ships to get ready for this coming fight."

"Thank you," Dalton said, again staring at his healthy hand, flexing it. "I'll try to repay this kindness."

"Just save us all, Doc," Brian said.

With that the three of them turned and left the lounge, stopping in the hallway outside.

With a wink to Dot, Brian signaled they were ready for transport, and a moment later he was in the hallway of his ship, *The Bad Business*, headed for the bridge.

If he had anything to say about it, he and Dot and the doctor would be enjoying drinks and dancing in that lounge very soon, celebrating their victory.

TWELVE

February 12th, 1961
Equivalent Earth Time
Location: Deep Space

BRIAN STROLLED INTO the Command Center of *The Bad Business* and dropped in to the big center chair facing a wall of screens. The Command Center was actually fairly small, with only four stations.

Usually his second-in-command, Marian Knudson, a stunning redhead from Wisconsin, sat in the chair to his left, but this time she had moved over to the communications chair directly behind him. Just from what little he knew so far of this mission, he needed someone he could trust at the communications station, especially since he had a hunch they were going over the border.

Marian knew that and had already moved. Carl Turner, the best navigator in the fleet was in the chair to his right.

"So what's happening, Captain?" Carl asked, his boyish face turning to look up at him. Brian could see that Carl was worried, not an emotion he normally showed in any way.

Carl appeared to be in his teens and had a face full of freckles. This far out, Carl was actually only twenty-one. Brian was twenty-eight or so. Carl was the youngest member of his crew, but Dot had a few slightly younger on her crew.

"From the best I can figure," Brian said, "and what little information I've been given, we're going to be getting a little younger. We have to take the fight to the Dogs."

"I hope I don't have to fly this thing in diapers," Carl said, shaking his head and turning back to his screens that surround his chair.

"We all hope that," Marian said from behind Brian.

Suddenly, across all the dozens of screens in the command center, an image of the area of space they were in came up. Admiral Lincoln's voice boomed out of the speaker, and Marian at the communications panel moved quickly to dampen it a little as Brian studied the three-dimensional chart on the big screen in front of him.

"Make sure everyone on the ship is getting this," Brian said to Marian and she nodded.

"The Dogs are on the verge of creating a new weapon," the admiral said over the image, "that will disconnect us all from this time and area of space and send us home."

Brian knew that much.

"They are within hours of launching the new weapon over the border and sending it toward Earth, followed by their fleet."

"Hours?" Carl said softly, then whistled under his breath.

Brian agreed with that shock. No wonder the brass had been in a hurry to extract everyone and get everyone staged. Brian had no idea there was so little time.

The screen showed the location of the *EPL* fleet, and then the location across the line that divided *EPL* space from Dog space. The weapon seemed to be on a big moon in a system three light years beyond the border.

"We're going to get five years younger if we go in there," Carl said, doing the quick math. "I'm going to have pimples again. Damn."

The illustration also showed a large fleet of Dog ships staging about four light years on the other side of the moon's system.

Brian didn't like the looks of that at all. *EPL* warships were far more powerful than Dog warships and had beat Dog ships before numbers of times. But *EPL* just didn't have enough ships out here on the edge to take on that entire fleet at once.

Not good, not good at all.

The admiral went on, not showing himself but instead just talking over the image of the ships and the moon with the weapon. "If we jump in and catch them by surprise, we'll only be outgunned about three-to-one around the weapon. But that Dog fleet will be coming in fast, so we won't have more than fifteen minutes at most."

"Ten," Brian said.

"Nine," Carl said.

Brian trusted Carl more than he trusted either the admiral or his own rough calculations.

"My first desire is to destroy everything on that moon," the admiral said, "including the weapon, but my science advisors warn me that if the weapon is functioning, that might set off a cascade effect. So we are going to let the science boys work on the problem of destroying the weapon for one more hour. Stand by at my command to jump in one hour."

At that his voice cut off, but the image of the border, the big moon, and the Dog fleet remained.

"I sure hope the guest we brought can come up with something," Brian said, staring at the impossible fight that they faced.

"Who's the guest?"

"Dr. Jack Dalton," Brian said.

Carl laughed. "This ought to be messing with his brain. Didn't he get discredited for even suggesting that all this is possible in physics?"

"He did," Brian said.

"Let's hope he's not bitter," Marian said.

THIRTEEN

February 12th, 1961
Equivalent Earth Time
Location: Deep Space

BRIAN SAT FOR the next forty-five minutes in his big command chair, not moving. There was just nothing he could do. Beside him Carl ran over calculations and in the fourth station Marian made sure all the ships were in close contact so they could work together when the fighting started.

Mostly Brian just stared at the area of battle and the space between here and there. He knew for a fact that the Dogs were watching the *EPL* fleet just as carefully.

At one point, two more of *EPL* warships appeared as late reinforcements.

Brian had no doubt that if every ship in the *EPL* fleet prepared to jump, the Dog fleet would do the same, and they would have even less time than the nine minutes Carl thought they all might have.

Brian slowly came to the conclusion that jumping the entire fleet at that moon just wouldn't work.

Suddenly, he knew what had to be done. "Marian, put me through to a private line with the admiral."

She smiled. "We're going in alone, aren't we?"

"Well, that would figure," Carl said. "Sounds like us."

Brian laughed, not wanting to tell her that she had guessed correctly. "Just put me through."

The admiral came on and said, "Yes, Captain."

The admiral clearly lived out here in this area of space, since his face was wrinkled and he showed his age. He hadn't come in from Earth. Brian had met him a few times after missions and never really had gotten a read on the admiral's age.

He had on full uniform, including his admiral's hat that looked more like a kid's hat with a long point, only made out of pure white cloth like the admiral's uniform. The hat actually looked almost silly.

"Has Doctor Dalton come up with anything yet?" Brian asked.

The admiral glanced over his shoulder, then turned back to the screen. "He believes a concentrated Electro-Magnetic-Pulse would shut the thing down safely and then conventional weapons could destroy it."

"If it's running, how close can we get?"

The admiral leaned forward and punched a board in front of him, showing the big moon. It took Brian a moment to see what the admiral was showing him.

"All the Dog ships are standing off, away from the planet," Brian said. "The thing is running."

"It would seem so," the admiral said, nodding, a grim look on his wrinkled face.

Brian nodded, then explained his plan and his reasons for it to the admiral.

"That will buy you all time back here," Brian said, "to rig up larger EMP weapons to stop it from a safe distance."

"Doctor Dalton believes the effects of the device will cover a sphere of two light years when launched and fully powered."

Now Brian was confused again. "Where is it going to get that kind of power?"

The admiral leaned back, then said abruptly, "I don't know. I'll be right back with you."

Beside Brian, Carl's fingers were moving at lightning speed over his board as the admiral's wrinkled old face was again replaced by the map.

"No sub-atomic reaction can produce that kind of energy," Carl said, "since the field it's generating would shut it down."

"They are using the moon as a spaceship," Brian said. "How big is that moon?"

"It's actually about the size of Earth's moon," Carl said.

"They are going to move something the size of the moon *and* power that weapon at the same time?" Brian asked. "That makes no sense without the very process they are shutting down."

Suddenly Carl and Brian looked at each other, smiling.

"They have a shield that protects their own power sources," Brian said.

"Which means, given time, we can develop shields as well," Carl said, smiling. "We just need to buy them time somehow."

"Exactly what I was thinking," Brian said, smiling at Carl.

Brian again signaled that Marian punch in a call to the admiral. As his face appeared, Brian said, "They have shields protecting their power sources."

"That's what Doctor Dalton just told me," the admiral said, smiling. "Can you buy us some time?"

"We are thinking exactly the same, Admiral. I'll be ready in ten minutes. Could you have Dalton send over targeting and frequency levels of the needed EMP blast?"

"I'll do one better. He'll join you in two minutes. And I'm sending *The Blooming Rose* with you. You'll run the first wave, she'll target with conventional weapons once you shut the thing down."

"Yes, sir," Brian said.

It always worried Brian when Dot went into any battle, but he had learned to click off the worry and just trust her. And it only took him a second to do that again.

He turned to Carl as the admiral's face vanished from the screen again. "Can we focus an EMP wave tight enough to target that weapon?"

"I'll have it ready in five," Carl said, his fingers again flying over the board.

Brian watched, amazed. He knew for a fact that Carl had lost both hands and one leg at seventy in a car wreck. Yet there he was moving so fast his fingers looked like a blur. It had to be really hard for him to go back to Earth after each mission, but never once had Brian heard Carl complain.

A moment later, Dr. Dalton appeared standing behind Carl, looking sort of stunned at the sudden change of location.

"They need to put a tingle or a noise on that transporter, don't they?" Brian said, standing and shaking the doctor's hand. "Great work."

"The other scientists did most of it," he said as Brian had him sit down in Marian's normal chair to Brian's left.

Brian introduced him to Carl and Marian, then Carl and Dalton quickly got to work on the calculations for the EMP blast.

"That's powerful enough to shut just about anything down in that weapon," the doctor said, nodding, "even if shielded from most EMP blasts. And that sudden shutdown will collapse the building subatomic field of the weapon."

"And if it *doesn't* shut it down and we bomb the thing?" Brian asked.

"With luck, nothing," Dalton said. "But it also might send a cascade wave through the area, in a radius of about ten light years. I suggested to the admiral that just as we are about to attack the weapon he move his fleet back four or five light years."

"Good idea," Brian said.

"Captain Leeds," Marian said, as Dot's face filled the screen in front of Brian.

"Captain," Brian said.

Dot smiled. "Captain. Are you ready?"

Brian glanced at Carl, and then at the doctor. Both nodded.

"Give the machine five seconds to shut down," Dalton said.

Dot nodded that she had heard. "We'll be exactly seven seconds behind you, on the same path. "Don't go stopping suddenly or we all might be in for a mess."

He laughed. "See you on the dance floor."

She smiled. "I don't know. My dance card is pretty full."

With that she clicked off.

That had been their ritual since their first night together dancing. So far it had pulled them through a lot of tight scrapes.

Brian clicked on the com link to the ship. "Be prepared to lay down covering fire for *The Blooming Rose* coming in behind us on my command. Stand by for jump."

Carl nodded. "Course plotted and in. You have exactly five seconds to fire after we appear near the weapon. We're going to be appearing right on the edge of those Dog warships standing off a distance from the weapon just to make sure we're not affected by it, either."

"So all hell is going to break loose," Brian said, nodding.

"With luck, we'll catch them by surprise," Carl said.

Marian's voice over the com-link counted down from five.

Five very, very long seconds.

"Engage," Marian said.

Carl's fingers flew over the panel and Brian took control of his ship.

A moment later they were five years farther out from Earth, and five years younger than they had been a moment before.

Around them was a small fleet of Dog warships, scattered in their standard, bowling-pin order, clearly just waiting to move.

Brian targeted the large area that was the weapon on the planet below, focusing down on the very center.

"Up the frequency ten percent," Dalton said, staring at the readings on the screen in front of him. "It's larger than we had calculated."

Carl's fingers flew, and an instant later he said, "Done."

Brian fired.

The invisible EMP blast hit the weapon base without any sort of impact.

Usually when Brian fired at something, things exploded. Not this time, but he kept firing anyway.

He could see that the Dog ships were turning, moving to attack. But it was taking them seconds, so they had been caught by surprise.

Dr. Dalton said, "The weapon is shutting down."

At that moment, a Dog warship opened fire, rocking the entire ship with two solid hits.

"Screens holding!" Carl said.

"Return fire!" Brian ordered over the shipboard com link.

He kept *The Bad Business* moving ahead as right behind them Dot's ship appeared and instantly started blasting the base. Her shots made an instant and clearly seen impact as the entire base started to shudder and explode.

"Covering fire for *The Blooming Rose*," Brian ordered all gunners.

Dot ignored all the fire she was taking from the Dogs, as all of her weapons were trained on the planet's surface.

"Our screens at sixty percent," Carl reported as more hits rocked them.

He kept his focus on the base below, holding the intense EMP blast on the weapon on the moon's surface.

"Blooming Rose's screens are at forty-two percent and holding," Carl reported, his voice calm.

Brian didn't know how long Dot's ship could hold out, but his gunners were doing a fantastic job of blowing up the closest Dog ships, creating a shield of exploding Dog ships for *The Blooming Rose*.

"Weapon is shut down," Dalton said, excitement clearly filling his voice.

Brian cut off the EMP blast and moved his ship closer to Dot's to help in the fight.

A moment later Dot stopped firing at the planet and began firing at the attacking ships. Brian could see from the readouts that *The Blooming Rose* had taken some damage, but Dot's screens were still holding.

"*The Blooming Rose* has done it," Carl said.

Brian snapped open a link to Dot.

"Let's go dancing," Brian said as her smiling face appeared.

A moment later, Carl jumped them out of the fight.

Brian just hoped Carl had jumped them in the right direction. He didn't think he could get much younger and he knew Carl couldn't.

They appeared right beside the *EPL* fleet at the point where the fleet had retreated in case the weapon had exploded.

A moment later *The Blooming Rose* appeared as well.

And Brian let out the breath he was holding.

On the view screen showing the Dogs' weapon moon, a fireworks display was happening; then after a moment, the Dog ships close to the planet jumped back to their own fleet.

And a few seconds later the moon exploded, looking like a small nova going off.

Wow, there had been a lot of energy on that planet.

"Are we safe, Doc?" Carl asked.

Doctor Dalton nodded, staring at the screen in front of him. "We are far enough away to not be bothered by that."

Brian glanced at Carl, then turned to the doctor. "So it worked?"

Dalton was still studying the readouts on the station in front of him, his thick eyebrows moving up and down as if they had a life of their own.

After a long moment, he turned and smiled, his huge eyebrows now up at the edge of his hairline. "It worked perfectly. I don't know about you, but I haven't felt this good in years."

"Yeah, space travel will do that for you," Carl said.

FOURTEEN

February 12th, 1961
Equivalent Earth Time
Location: Deep Space

DOT AND BRIAN came off the dance floor in the center of the large meeting room on the admiral's ship, laughing and both out of breath. Around them the dancers kept going, and the laughter filled the room louder than most parties.

The smells of the tables full of food against one wall still filled the air with ham and fresh bread. Not only had she danced too much, she had eaten too much, and maybe had a few too many drinks.

Everyone was happy tonight. And drinking.

She just felt happy to be alive. And with Brian.

Dot fanned herself, leaning against Brian. Even young, those fast songs of the 1950s and 1960s were work. She liked the slower ones. She had many very fond memories of slow dances from the earlier times, and with Brian in the last few years.

She still couldn't believe she could dance again. It was all such a dream at times.

They dropped down into chairs next to Dr. Dalton, who had just finished a conversation with Admiral Lincoln, who nodded to them as he left.

Dalton was smiling wider than she had ever seen a man smile before.

"So what's the great news?" Brian asked.

"Too much to believe," Dalton said, his smile getting ever bigger.

"You got to tell us before you explode," Dot said, laughing. It was a lot of fun to see a person so full of pure joy.

Dalton nodded and took a deep breath and then said quickly, "The admiral just got word from the *League* authorities that I will be allowed special permission, even though I am not married, to stay out here and continue my work as a young man again."

He said it so fast, he clearly couldn't believe it was true.

Dalton again opened and closed his hand, staring at it, clearly still stunned that he could do such a simple movement once again.

"Fantastic news," Doctor, Brian said.

"Wonderful, Doctor," Dot said, patting his arm. "The *EPL* needs you to help develop those screens."

"The admiral said I could continue my own work as well," Dalton said.

Dot smiled. She wondered what other fantastic things he would come up with, now that he had the freedom.

And the time.

And the belief in himself again.

"I have some applesauce to wear off," Brian said, smiling at Dot and pulling her to her feet.

She laughed at the impish grin on his handsome, young face, as a slow song started.

One thing about being young again with an old mind, you treasured every moment and every dance.

Right now, after escaping death once again, she wanted to treasure far more dances with the man of her dreams before she returned to that old body.

PART THREE

THE THIRD MAJOR MISSION

SIX MONTHS LATER

FIFTEEN

September 3rd, 2021
Actual Earth Time
Location: Chicago

THE YOUNG, STRONG Lieutenant Kennison gently nudged Captain Brian Saber in his nursing home bed, pulled back the light brown blanket and sheet covering him, and then easily picked Brian up with strong arms.

Brian was going on a mission.

Brian could feel the excitement surge through his old body yet again.

A mission, a chance to live again, to be young again.

He made himself take as deep a breath as he could without setting off a fit of coughing. His stroke-crippled body just couldn't take much at this point, but the promise of a mission always got him excited.

The Shady Valley Nursing Home room hadn't changed since Brian fell asleep at 10 p.m. Now his old clock on the wall told him it was a little after one in the morning. If he survived this mission, he would be

77

back in fifteen minutes. But he might be out there in space for a month or more, if he was lucky.

The young lieutenant turned for the room's sliding glass door. Behind him Brian caught a glimpse of Captain Dorothy "Dot" Leeds being carried from her room across the hall and into his room by Lieutenant Sherri.

She followed Brian and Lieutenant Kennison out into the night air of a Chicago late summer night. The air was thick and heavy and the smell of freshly mowed grass surprised him.

The light nightshirt Brian wore to bed was almost too much for the warm night. He used to love being out in nights like this when he was younger and married. Now it made it hard for him to breathe, but he wouldn't be out in the humid, thick air long enough for it to matter.

Overhead, he could see the full moon, bright in the night sky. He and Dot were both far too old to ever walk under that moon, even on a warm night. But at some point in the near future, he hoped they would be together, staring up at some moon, somewhere in this sector of space.

No one talked.

He could hardly speak anymore, but none of the other three bothered either. It was all business for all of them.

They were on a mission.

Around the country right now his crew, and Dot's crew, were going through the same routine.

Damn he was excited.

He always felt this way going on a mission.

The four of them neared the center of the courtyard of the nursing home. He could feel the humidity forming slight sweat on his face and neck, but there was nothing he could do to wipe it away.

The full moon was so beautiful on a clear summer night. He hoped he would see it again later.

Then a yellow beam struck them from above and lifted all four of them up easily into the big intergalactic transport ship.

The cooler, thinner air of the ship covered him and behind him he heard Dot say softly, "See you on the other side."

He would have answered her, but he couldn't talk louder than a whisper at a good moment. He couldn't walk or even lift his arms at all either. A stroke a little over a year ago had taken most of those skills.

She knew that and didn't expect an answer from him.

They were both very much in love.

At some point soon he hoped to ask her to marry him and live out on the frontier, not ever having to return to earth and their old bodies. He hadn't gotten around to it yet, but hoped to very soon.

She hadn't brought it up either, but he knew she was just old-fashioned enough to not do that. And since they hadn't talked about it, he wasn't sure if she understood the rules of living out at the edge of the *EPL* space. They really needed to talk about it.

And he needed to flat ask her to marry him.

But right now they were still frontline fighters. And clearly they were needed.

Lieutenant Kennison put Brian down in his sleep coffin in a private cabin off to one side of the big hallway and stepped back and snapped off a salute. "Good luck, sir," he said.

Then he lowered the lid until it latched over Brian and the light went out.

Brian would have loved to salute the young man back, but he couldn't. He couldn't even wipe off the drip of sweat threatening to run into his right eye.

Instead, he just lay there thinking of seeing Dot again in her young and youthful body.

And he thought of them dancing as they always did after a mission.

But first they had to survive whatever faced them in deep space this time.

A faint orange and rose smell seeped into the coffin and Captain Brian Saber dozed off.

SIXTEEN

September 3rd, 1961
Equivalent Earth Time
Location: Deep Space

BRIAN AWOKE WHAT seemed like just an instant later.

He reached up and easily pushed the coffin lid open. Then he levered his young body out of the sleep chamber.

He never got tired of that feeling after being trapped in that wheelchair and bed what seemed like just moments before. The magic of the Trans-Galactic speed had done it to him again, given him his young body back.

He had sure taken this body for granted when he had been young. He didn't now. Not for a moment.

The memory of his stroke-beaten body was always just too fresh in his mind when he was in this younger body.

He quickly slipped off the old nightshirt and tossed it back in the coffin. He would need that for the return trip back.

If he survived.

He pushed that thought away.

If he didn't, his son would be called in the middle of the night and there would be a funeral for a body that looked like his old body that was a fake. And no one but those in the *Earth Protection League* would know Brian Saber of Chicago died in space, fighting for the safety of all humanity.

And Brian didn't honestly care if anyone knew. He just loved doing this, getting a chance to be young again.

This trip they must have gone a little farther out in distance from Earth. He looked to be about twenty-five. Often he ended up closer to thirty on missions.

So that meant they were very, very close to the *EPL* border, more than likely the border with the Dogs.

He quickly dressed, then with one last look in the mirror as he always did, he left his room, turning right and heading for the command center.

He was on his own warship, *The Bad Business*.

Dot would have been transferred to her ship as well, *The Blooming Rose*. He wished he could see her now, kiss her, hold her with his young strong arms. But there would be time for that later.

Right now he had to focus on the mission they faced, whatever it was.

He got to the Command Center just a few seconds before his other two command crew arrived.

Marian Knudson, took her second chair to his left and started working on the boards in front of her, bringing up the screens in the command center to show the area of space they were in. The two of them had been a team for years now.

She was tough, all business, and smart as they came.

This time she had her red hair long and down over her shoulders. Usually she kept it up tight against her head.

Behind them Carl dropped into his chair with a "Damn this feels good. Home again."

Brian felt the same way.

The small command center with its four chairs and many screens and control boards was his home.

"I like my home on Earth," Marian said.

Back in Wisconsin, Marian lived alone, even at the age of ninety, in her own home. As Carl had said once, she was too damn mean to die or live anywhere else.

Marian had not argued with that, only smiled that smile that let Brian know that at some point Carl would pay for the remark.

"So any news as to the mission, Captain?" Marian asked, her fingers running over the board in front of her. "We are within striking distance of the Dog border. Much closer than normal, actually, which is why Carl here has pimples. No sign at all of Dog warships."

"There are six other *EPL* ships with us," Carl said. "One is *The Blooming Rose.*"

Everyone knew about his and Dot's relationship. They had made no attempt at all to keep it a secret. There had been no point and no one had seemed to care.

"No word yet," Brian said. "But I suspect we don't have long to wait."

He pointed to the board in front of him, and as he did, a red light started blinking, meaning an emergency message was coming in.

"You creep me out every time you do that," Carl said, shaking his head and turning back to his board.

Brian just smiled at Marian. The brass had a certain timetable that they allowed the crews to get into positions on their ships, and that timetable never varied, so Brian always knew when the message was coming in.

"Message on screen," Carl said a moment later.

General Holmes's face appeared, his frown causing his middle-aged face to wrinkle even more than it already was. His hair was balding and he looked like he had recently seen too much sun on that exposed skin.

They had worked a few times with General Holmes. He was in charge of the defense forces in the ground bases scattered along the *EPL* borders.

"Captains," he said, nodding. "I'm afraid this is as bad as it gets."

Brian said nothing, as did the other captains of the other six warships, so the general went on.

"The Dogs have launched a moon at Earth."

Brian sat there hoping that General Holmes would take back that statement.

He didn't.

The general just kept frowning.

"The moon is accelerating from deep in Dog space and will be at the border at your position in about six hours."

"Fleet of ships with it I assume?" Saber asked.

The general shook his head. "They don't think they need ships on this one. The moon they have launched is as big as our moon around Earth. It's not carrying a weapon like they tried last time. The moon is the weapon."

Brian sat back and tried to imagine what it would take to get a moon like that actually moving, what kind of power and how the moon would even hold together. And how they would even aim it from such a long distance through space.

And how many thousands of years at real-space travel it would take to get to Earth.

"I'm sending all the data we have on it through to all of you," the general said. "We want you to investigate the moon the moment it crosses into our space, pass on the data to our scientists on bases closer to Earth."

With that he clicked off, leaving the screen blank.

"Why do I think there's something he flat omitted from that briefing," Carl said.

Marian's fingers flew over her board as Brian sat there, waiting. He knew Carl was right. The General wasn't telling them everything. There was something more.

"Oh, shit," Marian said.

Brian looked over at her. She never swore.

She put up the report that made her swear on the main screen in front of Brian so that they could all see it.

"One hour after the moon crosses into our space," Marian said, "it reaches Trans-Galactic speed and will be protected by the Trans-Galactic shields. Nothing will be able to change its course until it plows into Earth."

"They built a T-G drive big enough to power a moon at full speed," Carl said, shaking his head. "Wow! That's impressive. So how about we just stop it like we did the last time they tried to launch a moon?"

Brian had to admit, it was impressive. But there was only one problem. Once something was in Trans-Galactic drive, it couldn't be stopped. It wasn't in real time and the shields that formed with the drive could plow through anything.

So they had to figure out a way to stop a speeding moon before it got up to speed completely.

Or Earth would be destroyed very, very shortly.

SEVENTEEN

September 3rd, 1961
Equivalent Earth Time
Location: Deep Space

BRIAN LOOKED AROUND at his command crew, then shook his head. "Looks like we got seven hours to figure this out. Marian, make sure to get that report to everyone on board who understand Trans-Galactic drive physics."

Marian nodded, her fingers moving quickly over the controls as Brian swiveled his big chair completely around so he could see Carl on his right and Marian on his left in the small command center.

Actually he was facing the door, but since his chair was slightly ahead of theirs at point in the room, they could all talk this way. His back was to his screens, but they could still access their screens while they talked.

"Done," she said.

Brian knew that meant the other thirty-some members of his crew all knew the score and were working on solutions as well. When you had that many experienced people working hard on something, results tended to happen.

And Brian knew that everyone on the other ships were doing the same. That was a lot of years experience focused on the same problem. One of the advantages of having a lot of really old minds in young bodies.

"Let me kind of think out loud here," Brian said.

Both Marian and Carl nodded.

"I assume T-G space will power the thing once the moon reaches hyperspace speed. But what's powering it now?"

Both Carl and Marian had the report at their fingertips and it was Marian who spoke first. "The moon has a hot core, so the engines spaced around the moon are feeding off the internal core of the moon itself."

"All T-G engines," Carl said. "Are shielded from EMP blasts as would be expected since we toasted their last moon. Nothing we have will knock them out."

Brian knew that and he nodded. He'd been in a lot of fights with Dog warships and knocking their engines out was never an option, just as Dogs knocking out a T-G *EPL* engine wasn't possible either. It was the nature of Trans-Galactic engines and the force fields that built up around them.

"Can we dig the engines out of the moon's surface outside the shields?" Brian asked.

Again both his command crew worked on the report, then both shook their heads at the exact same time. "Engines are buried thirty miles deep inside the moon. No dislodging them."

Brian looked at the big screen near Carl with the report and wondered how the *EPL* got all the information. More than likely a number of good people had died for it.

"And I assume no blowing the moon apart before it enters Trans-Galactic speed?" Brian asked.

"They found the most stable hunk of rock I've ever seen," Carl said and Marian nodded.

"It would take an entire fleet of ships," Carl said, sounding disgusted, "pounding it with all weapons, and I doubt that even that much would make more than a dent."

They all three sat there in silence. Brian just kept looking around, looking at his young body, at his command crew's young bodies. Somehow they had made it out here, to this exact location in space.

And suddenly he knew that was the key to this.

He looked at Carl. "Who is driving the moon?"

"No one will be on the moon," Carl said, looking at the report.

"So who drives us when we come out here," Brian asked. "Who gets us to exact coordinates, with Trans-Galactic drives, in those transport ships."

Marian frowned and turned back to her board.

Carl did the same thing.

Brian knew he was on to something and something important. You don't just send a ship hurtling through more miles of space than Brian wanted to think about without something or someone driving. Even with top shields, you didn't want to plow holes through things along the way that didn't need holes in them.

So those transport ships from Earth had someone driving it, controlling it, from somewhere.

And that moon would have someone driving all the way to Earth. One planet that far away was far, far too small a target to hit from over sixty light years of distance without a number of course corrections along the way.

"Computers," Marian finally said. "Each transport we take out here is run by a computer to do course corrections."

"Through sensors, the computer is able to see the route ahead," Carl said, "and make corrections to avoid the transport putting a hole in something else along the way."

"So there is a computer on that moon somewhere?" Brian asked. "We know where?"

"Buried with the Trans-Galactic drive engines," Marian said quickly.

"Damn," Carl said, clearly getting angry. "They thought of everything."

"Not everything," Brian said, smiling. "Is the moon rotating in any fashion?"

Carl and Marian both looked puzzled at him, then quickly checked.

"No," Marian said. "It couldn't rotate and maintain its T-G drive thrust."

"So we blind it," Brian said. "Tough to hit anything without being able to see."

"The computer sensors," Carl said, laughing. "Of course, they would have to be hidden on the front side of the moon to feed the computer."

"And I'll wager those sensors are not hardwired into that computer," Brian said. "Not through that much rock."

Marian laughed, the first time Brian had heard that for some time. "What are you thinking, Captain?"

"We going to just blow those sensors off the face of the moon?" Carl asked.

Brian sat back, his hands behind his head, smiling. "I have a better idea."

"Oh, I love it when he smiles like that," Carl said, laughing.

"How about," Brian said, "we feed those computers in that moon some bad targeting information, something simple such as the location of a big Dog military base."

"Oh, that will annoy them something awful," Carl said, laughing so hard tears were coming to his eyes.

Marian informed all the other ships of the idea and then all three of them set to work on exactly where on that moon those sensors would be planted and how to intercept the signal from the surface sensors to the moon targeting computer.

The fallback plan was to wipe all the sensors from the face of the moon and hope it missed Earth. But Brian liked his plan a lot better, and didn't let that moon even get into *EPL* space.

EIGHTEEN

September 3rd, 1961
Equivalent Earth Time
Location: Deep Space

THE MOON WAS fast approaching the *EPL* border when *Earth Protection League* Command gave the clearance to try their plan. It had been a scientist on Dot's ship who had finally cracked the Dog computer code between the moon targeting computer and the sensors.

And it had been a scientist on yet another warship who had figured out how to intercept the signals from the sensors.

They needed to have a ship in tight over each of the six sensors on the moon and the intercept would have to be sent at exactly the same moment to all sensors.

In essence, the control of the moon was going to be transferred to Brian. He and Carl and Marian were going to turn the moon just before it started into Trans-Galactic drive and fire it at a Dog military base.

And then destroy the targeting computer with a very nasty virus.

That moon would wipe out that Dog base and then head out into deep space at full T-G drive. The engines would have to fail before that moon dropped back into normal space a very, very long ways away from this entire galaxy.

At least that was the plan.

But there was one major problem with the plan that Brian didn't much like. Six *EPL* ships would have to basically hover in close over the moon to intercept the signal from each sensor and relay the signal to his ship and then, in turn, take the new instructions and feed them back into the sensors.

Dot and her ship would be one of those in close. They would have to stay in close during the moon's turn and then somehow get a safe distance away when the moon jumped to Trans-Galactic Drive.

It was going to take exact timing. Just a second or two of delay and a warship would be lost.

And if one warship didn't stay in close enough, all six sensors wouldn't feed the computer the right data and there was no telling what might happen.

Brian sat back in his chair, trying to keep his nerves under control as they waited the last ten minutes. He knew everyone was busy checking and double-checking the plan. He had talked with Dot privately thirty minutes before, telling her to be careful and that he loved her.

She just laughed that wonderful, young laugh of hers, and said, "Trust me, I'm not missing the dancing tonight for anything."

Dot loved to dance, more than anything in life it seemed at times.

And he loved to dance with her.

"Moon crossing the border now, Captain," Marian said.

Brian nodded to Carl who opened a fleet-wide communications link.

"Move into positions now."

On the screen in front of him Brian could see the six other *EPL* warships with their sleek noses and wing-like appearance move as one, turning toward the large moon and matching speed with it.

EPL warships had been designed to look like birds not only to allow them atmospheric flight if needed, but because in so many of the cultures the *EPL* fought against, birds were feared.

Including with the Dogs.

Brian kept *The Bad Business* outside and above the group, moving with them to match the speed of the moon.

They all looked very small against the huge size of the moon, like real birds hovering over a large open area.

Then, almost as a practiced dance in space, the six ships broke away from each other and moved in over an area of the large moon.

The closer it got, Brian could see that it did look a great deal like their moon at home. It had no atmosphere and was covered with impact craters. And it was just about the same size.

Brian took *The Bad Business* in right over the center of the moon and matched the moon's speed and acceleration to stay in position.

"Thirty seconds," Marian said.

"Signal when in position," Brian ordered the other ships.

Each ship had to hover no more than a football field length above the surface where the sensor was, and match the increasing speed of the moon at the same time.

Very, very tricky flying and a slight miss and the *EPL* warship would crash into the moon's surface, or be too far away to intercept the signal.

Brian could see *The Blooming Rose* turn and settle into its assigned position above the moon surface. Dot would be flying it.

She had one of the steadiest hands at the helm of a ship that he had ever seen.

Three other warships signaled ready.

Then Dot signaled *The Blooming Rose* was in position and steady.

"Ready here," Brian said, checking to make sure his people were ready with the computer download and new signal into the moon's computer.

At the same moment the other two ships reported they were in position and stable.

"Hold and be ready to turn with the moon," Brian said.

"Intercept signal," Brian ordered the other ships.

As one all turned green that they had the sensor signal.

Then he turned to Marian. "Feed it."

Her fingers flew over the panel and the new programming for the Dog's computer was fed through all six sensors.

An instant later the moon started to turn off its course for Earth.

"Stay with it, everyone," Brian commanded to the other ships as he moved *The Bad Business* to maintain position and keep the feed to the other ships constant.

The moon kept turning and somehow the *EPL* warships held their positions.

"We got some swearing and close calls," Carl said, "but everyone's holding."

"Ten more seconds," Marian said. "And the virus will be loaded."

At five seconds Brian counted it down for the other Captains.

"Five. Four. Three. Two. One."

Marian signaled cut.

"Get out of there now!" Brian shouted to the other pilots.

As one, the other pilots moved their ships up and away from the rough surface of the moon.

Brian had *The Bad Business* moving with them, pushing the ship as fast as he could to try to reach a safe distance.

Twenty seconds later the moon vanished into Trans-Galactic drive space, headed back into the Dog's territory and right for a large military base.

"Clear," Carl said. "All ships made it out of the wash zone from the drive."

Brian slumped in his chair, just smiling as both Carl and Marian applauded and laughed.

Somehow, Earth had dodged that moon.

Barely.

NINETEEN

September 3rd, 1961
Equivalent Earth Time
Location: Deep Space

BRIAN LOOKED DOWN into the wonderful brown eyes of Dot and smiled. "One more dance?"

Around them the music of the last slow song had just died off and a few remaining crew members from other ships were slowly working their way toward the doors that led to the transport ship. The huge ballroom that had been an ongoing party for days was now mostly empty.

She laughed, the sound high and wonderful and something he needed to remember in the long days and nights at the nursing home.

"Our bus is going to leave without us," she said after kissing him quickly.

"Let it," he said, pulling her close and enjoying the feel of her against him.

Since they had turned the moon weapon back on the Dogs, the

general had allowed all seven *EPL* warships to dock at Stevens Base for some well-deserved time off while in younger bodies.

Brian and Dot had spent the first night dancing until they had no energy left to even drag themselves out onto the floor.

They had gone back to his room on the base and found a lot more energy. The next day they had spent in meetings with the general and others, then dancing more that evening, then back to her room for the night.

He kissed her again, then together they turned and walked hand-in-hand to the big double doors of the large room, not saying anything.

In fact, they said nothing all the way down the corridor that seemed to stretch for a good mile, then up into their transport. He just wanted to enjoy her company and walking with her.

He needed to remember it all.

He kissed Dot one more time at her cabin door.

"Help me with my applesauce in the morning?" he asked

She smiled. "Always."

Then like two kids saying goodnight after a date in high school, she stepped inside and closed the door.

He walked slowly to his cabin and took off his uniform.

He loved putting it on every mission. He hated taking it off because that meant he wouldn't be young.

He wanted to stay young, to keep serving Earth and defending the *League*.

Going back to his old body was part of that, but not a part he liked.

He slipped back into his old nightshirt and crawled into the coffin-like chamber and pulled the lid closed.

The next thing he remembered, he was being lifted by Lieutenant Kennison from his sleep chamber.

His old stroke-damaged body now part of him again.

Dot and Lieutenant Sherri met them at the transport chamber.

Brian so wanted to reach out to touch Dot's hand, but he could no longer move his arms hardly at all.

The warm thick, humid air of the Chicago night hit him as the transport beam let them go in the nursing home center court.

Above him the golden moon was full in the late summer night air.

He stared up at it as the lieutenant carried him toward his room.

"Not so pretty any more, is it?" Dot said softly from behind him.

She was right.

It wasn't.

After this mission, he wasn't sure if he would ever look up at the moon in the same way again.

It was amazing how seeing the universe and defending Earth could change a person's perspective on things in such a short time.

Simple things like staring up at the moon.

PART FOUR
THE LAST MISSION

SEVEN MONTHS LATER

TWENTY

April 19th, 2022
Actual Earth Time
Location: Chicago

DOT PUSHED HER wheelchair ahead of her into the breakfast room of Shady Valley Nursing Home. The big room where she and Brian ate three of their meals every day smelled like pancakes and eggs this fine clear spring day. One morning she had come in and actually smelled bacon, but that had only been a special treat for one resident on his birthday.

She had never liked bacon that much, but the smell had been heavenly.

She liked the warm feeling of the room full of twenty tables set up like a restaurant. Outside the open windows and brown drapes that were tied back and open, she could see the spring starting to bloom on Chicago, and the sun was shining, putting everyone in a light mood.

It felt like the long winter was over.

She could feel it as well.

She got most of the way to her normal table, pushing her wheel-chair ahead of her through the obstacle course of the tables and chairs, when she looked up and realized Brian wasn't in his place yet.

Her stomach twisted slightly at the empty place where the nurse would wheel Brian up in his wheelchair and tuck a bib on him. Then three meals a day Dot would help feed him.

It always amazed her how much she loved that man, both in his old form and when he was young, the handsome Captain Brian Saber, and they were in deep space fighting for the survival of Earth.

What mattered to her was that incredible brain and his strength and caring. Old body or young body, she loved Brian.

She had never thought she would find love again in her life. But she had and now just having him late for breakfast bothered her more than she wanted to admit.

When Janice, the orderly, brought her normal two eggs, two pancakes, and orange juice, Dot asked her, "Where's Brian?"

He's a little under the weather this morning," Janice said, "so he's still in bed.

Alarm bells went off in Dot's mind and her stomach twisted into a knot. If Brian died here, from another stroke, or a heart attack, she would lose him forever.

That stroke that had taken the last of his movement a year or so ago had scared her more than she wanted to think about right now. He had survived it, but barely. Another one like that he wouldn't survive.

It was one thing to watch his ship go into battle because she knew that if he died in battle, defending Earth, he wouldn't mind.

But he couldn't die of old age in a nursing home. Not the great Captain Brian Saber, the most decorated Captain ever in the history of the *Earth Protection League*.

She left most of her breakfast and headed back down the hall toward their rooms. Her room was across the hall from his and it hadn't occurred to her to see if he was there when she left.

She hurried as fast as her damaged legs would allow her, pushing her wheelchair ahead of her. The trip down the hallway seemed to stretch, but eventually she got to his door and eased it open.

His room was dark and she could hear his labored breathing.

"Oh, thank God," she said softly to herself.

He was covered by a sheet, and his frail, old body seemed tiny on the large hospital bed.

She moved into the room silently, letting the door close gently behind her, dropping the room into a dimness lit only by the nightlight from the open bathroom door.

She moved over beside him and brushed his rough cheek gently.

He didn't wake up.

She sat in her wheelchair, facing his bed.

This was where she belonged.

At his side.

TWENTY-ONE

April 20th, 2022
Actual Earth Time
Location: Chicago

"CAPTAIN LEEDS," the young, female voice said in a very gentle tone.

There was a mission tonight. Oh, thank heavens. She would get to see Brian again and talk with him about what they were going to do to get him out of the nursing home before another stroke took him from her.

She had sat all day, off and on, beside his bed as he slept, only leaving to use the bathroom and go to lunch and then dinner.

But at both she hadn't felt like eating much at all. It wasn't the same sitting there without Brian.

Finally, Joyce, the night nurse, had woken her early in the evening since she had fallen asleep in her wheelchair beside Brian, her head on his bed beside him. The nurse had convinced her to go to bed even though she didn't want to leave Brian's side.

Lieutenant Sherri picked up Dot in her strong arms and moved quickly, but carefully, across the hall and into Brian's room, then toward the sliding glass door that led into the center courtyard.

Brian was still in the bed, sleeping.

"Isn't Captain Saber coming on this mission?"

"He is not," Sherri said. "I honestly don't know why."

Dot felt her stomach twist into a knot and she almost told Sherri to put her back to bed. She had never gone on a mission without Brian and she didn't want this to be the first.

"Stop for a moment, Lieutenant," Dot said, her voice firm and almost an order. Sherri did as instructed.

Dot needed a moment to think this through.

She glanced at Brian's old wall clock that ticked like a bomb, filling his room with a constant reminder of time passing.

Three-sixteen in the morning.

She would be back shortly in Earth time. Maybe fifteen or twenty minutes at the most, even though she might spend days or weeks on the mission. Somehow the weirdness of the space travel could bring her back just a short time after she left.

So she wouldn't be gone that long in nursing home time.

Brian seemed to be resting peacefully, his breathing normal. Maybe it was right to not stress him with a mission and tire him out even more if he wasn't feeling well.

Plus, if she left for these few minutes, it would allow her to talk with someone in the *League*, get them to get Brian out of here before he died. Surely there was something the most decorated captain in the *Earth Protection League* could do in deep space in a young, healthy body.

So going on the mission would be her best chance to help Brian. She would talk with someone as soon as the mission was over.

If she lived, that was.

If some alien didn't kill her first.

"I'm ready," Lieutenant," she said with one long look at Brian.

She had once figured up that in the last four years of going on missions, she had actually got to live another fourteen years of life in space, young again. And every extra minute had been wonderful. Scary at times, but wonderful.

And all of it had been with Brian.

The first year, until she earned her own ship, she had served on Brian's ship.

They had danced so many times.

She didn't want that to end now.

She wouldn't let it if she had anything to say about it.

The sliding door to the outside slid silently open and the Chicago early spring air bit hard against her old skin. Lieutenant Sherri didn't even pause at the door other than to slide it quickly and silently closed.

They were only in the cold air for a moment before a yellow beam of light lifted them both quickly into the transport ship that was cloaked above the nursing home.

Dot knew that around the country the same thing had happened, or was happening, at least forty-one other times as the crew of *The Blooming Rose* was gathered from their perspective nursing homes and retirement apartments. A couple of them even lived in the same nursing home, which General Brooks had once said made things a lot easier, but was too dangerous for the most part to have more than two because if their entire ship was lost, the league didn't want to try to explain why half of the population of a nursing home died suddenly one night.

She couldn't imagine going on missions without Brian there as well to talk with. Although for years before she had known about the league, he had gone on missions and not told her a word.

Lieutenant Sherri quickly carried Dot down the hallway in the ship to a room with a silver, coffin-shaped sleep chamber and laid Dot down slowly on the soft cushions inside.

Dot loved the symbol of the coffin allowing her to be young again. It made her smile every time.

The young lieutenant patted her shoulder. "Have a good trip, Captain."

Then she closed the lid on the coffin and tapped it twice as a signal to Dot that it was secure. In this old body, it didn't matter. Dot wouldn't have been able to even push the lid open if she tried.

A moment later the orange and rose-smelling gas filled the chamber and she drifted off into the sleep of the dead.

Her coffin would be transferred to her ship *The Blooming Rose* with the rest of her crew in deep space.

Only then would she discover what was so important as to pull her away from the man she loved.

TWENTY-TWO

April 20th, 1962
Equivalent Earth Time
Location: Deep Space

THE TOP OF the coffin snapped open with a hiss and cool oxygen bathed over her face. Captain Dot Leeds snapped her eyes open, then held her arms up to look at them. What she saw was the young skin and shapes of youth.

She flexed her fingers and the muscles under the skin rippled.

It felt wonderful.

It always felt wonderful.

No pain, no aches.

Just the sense of health and youth.

She had made it again.

The room smelled faintly of oranges and roses mingled with machine oil, and she loved both smells. She had called her ship *The Blooming Rose* because of that smell.

With both hands, she grabbed the sides of the coffin sleep module and lifted herself out, kicking over the side without so much as a caught heel. The feeling of youth was simply wonderful, better than any drug ever invented.

She still wore her old woman's nightgown, but she quickly pulled that off and tossed it back in the coffin. She would need it for the return trip, if she lived through this coming fight. If not, they'd need it for her body. And tomorrow morning her son on the west coast would get a call that she had died peacefully in her sleep.

But she had no plans on dying this mission. She wouldn't do that to Brian. She wouldn't leave him there alone to die in his old body. That wasn't going to happen.

She flexed the muscles in her shoulders and neck. Her body was one she barely remembered from her youth. Yet each time she went on a mission, this body returned, good as ever. Whatever the strange relative-matter-physics involved in Trans-Galactic travel, she loved this body, and hadn't appreciated it enough back when she was young.

At least she hadn't appreciated it in the right ways.

She got dressed and then brushed a hand through her now full head of brown hair. Then she turned and glanced at the only mirror in the small room.

The reflection that greeted her was one of her youth, control, and power. She couldn't be more than twenty-one or twenty-two on this mission. Only the knowledge and memories inside the young body were of an eighty-seven year old woman who had, seemingly moments before, been asleep in a nursing home room in Chicago, on the planet Earth.

No telling exactly where in space she was at the moment.

She looked twenty-one, but was a four-year veteran of the *Earth Protection League*. Earth time.

She had earned her ship and her captain's rank faster than even Brian had done. Brian's advice and guidance had been amazing and part of that quick rise to being a Captain.

One nice thing about being in the *EPL*. Out here it didn't matter how young you looked. Just that you got the job done.

She patted the stunner on her hip, enjoying the solid feel of the hard-rubber handle. Years ago she never would have thought she could ever fire a gun, let alone enjoy feeling one on her hip.

With one more quick look in the mirror, she turned and strode out of the room, turning right toward the Command Center of *The Blooming Rose*.

She had a mission to finish and people to talk to before getting back to Brian and getting him out of that nursing home.

She knew this ship like the back of her now-young hand. She had been on board it for almost a hundred missions, had renamed it when she became captain, had flown it through some of the toughest space in this sector of the Galaxy. It felt like home, far more than her home back in Chicago had ever done. In fact, her cabin on this ship was twice the size as her nursing home room.

The hallways of the ship were wide enough that three people could walk side-by-side. The metal walls were covered in a rubber coating and painted light blue which made them feel warm and soft and inviting, not like walking down the corridor of a normal military ship.

She also loved the floors. They were all coated in a thicker rubber substance that kept noise down and were still solid under a person's feet. Only problem was that one person could sneak up on another easily.

Every twenty paces was a communications screen on the wall for instant contract from anywhere in the ship and every forty paces was a sliding bulkhead door hidden in the walls that could be closed to shut off sections of the ship.

Throughout the ship her crew would be coming awake in their cabins, dressing and moving to their stations, getting ready for whatever faced them on this mission.

She didn't wait for them, but instead strode directly to the empty Command Center and dropped down into the captain's chair.

Her chair.

Around her the fairly small room was only three other stations, one on her left, the other on her right, both with a high-backed chair like hers and view screens above them showing the blackness of space and seven other *EPL* warships.

The fourth station was behind her, the communication station. She never had anyone in that spot, letting her two command crew do that job.

Brian did the same on his ship.

Actually, the Command Center was on the very front and highest point of the warship. And the ship itself was so big that even at a good pace it was a good five-minute hike from the Command Center to the engine room at the back of the warship.

And the ship itself, as all *EPL* battleships, was shaped like a bird. It seemed that many of Earth's enemies found birds frightening creatures.

In front of her a small screen on the panel flared to light and the smiling face of General George Meyers filled it. He had deep blue eyes, white hair, and more wrinkles than almost any human Dot had ever seen. Yet the face was one that seemed comfortable with command. She had no idea where he was located, in what part of space. For all she knew, he could be back on Earth, but she didn't think so.

"Glad you made it, Captain Leeds."

"Glad to be here, sir," Dot said. "I'm going to need to talk with you about Captain Saber after this is finished."

The General nodded. "Of course."

"So what is the problem?"

She expected the normal mission briefing, but was shocked when the General said, "Not yet. I need you to gather with seven other Captains on Captain Saber's ship. His second in command, Marian Knudson has the helm for this mission."

"When?" Dot asked.

She had spent a lot of time on Brian's ship, but never once when he wasn't on it.

"Twenty minutes," he said and the screen went blank.

"What was that all about?" Steve "Quick Draw" Oldham asked as he dropped into his chair in the station to her right.

Steve was her second-in-command and had been her close friend for years now, even turning down his own ship to stay with her as a team. He lived in a nursing home in California somewhere. On Earth he was three years younger than she was. He looked like a teenager on this mission. It seems they had really pushed them out farther away from Earth than normal.

Steve had gotten his nickname in basic camp because he could draw a photon stunner faster than even the instructor and was a deadly shot with it. Watching too many Roy Rogers westerns when he was a kid, he had said. The nickname had stuck.

"Not a clue," Dot said, shaking her head.

She didn't like having to get with other captains and without Brian to lead them. It meant something real ugly was happening.

She stood as her third-in-command came in.

Carrie Nelson lived in the Chicago area as well, but out near the airport, and was about Dot's age on Earth. Out in space she was a petite little blonde who couldn't be more than five-two at best. Dot at five-six seemed to tower over her.

Yet Dot had seen Carrie in a fight. She was like a whirlwind and if Dot had to pick Steve or Carrie to have her back when things got ugly in hand-to-hand, she would pick Carrie.

"A little meeting first," Dot said to Carrie's puzzled look. "Got to go over to Captain Saber's ship."

She smiled. "Not too much time I hope."

Captain Saber is not along on this mission," Dot said. "Not feeling well."

"Oh," was all Carrie said, looking at Dot with a compassionate look.

"Don't worry," Dot said, smiling at her friend and third-in-command. "I'll get his ass out of that nursing home when we get done here."

"So who's driving *The Bad Business?*" Steve asked.

"Marian Knudson is acting Captain," Dot said.

"I hear she's a red-headed dream on two legs," Carrie said, laughing and winking at Dot. "You should take Steve along. He needs to get laid once before he dies."

Steve put his hand up in the air. "I volunteer for that duty."

Dot shook her head. "I have a hunch Acting Captain Knudson makes it a habit to not sleep with anyone with Quick in their reputation."

She winked at Carrie who could barely contain her laughter with her back to Steve's frown.

"Get the ship up and ready to go," Dot said, smiling at her two friends. "I'll be back shortly. I have a hunch we're in some deep trouble with this mission."

And whatever they were facing, she was going to beat it and get back to Earth and Brian, one way or another.

TWENTY-THREE

April 20th, 1962
Equivalent Earth Time
Location: Deep Space

DOT STOPPED BESIDE the other six captains, all of whom she already knew well, as Acting-Captain Knudson walked to the front of the room that the crew used for mostly dances and watching movies.

Dot and Brian had spent a lot of time in this room after missions, dancing and talking.

Right now the big movie screen had been extended from the wall and everyone was facing the screen.

The silence in the room felt like that of a funeral. Dot just hoped it wasn't going to be all of their funerals they were attending.

Marian clicked the intercom. "Go ahead, Carl."

A moment later General Bank's face filled the big screen. The General didn't wear his normal smile as he said, "Good morning, captains. We have an ugly situation at hand."

Dot stood back to one side and tried to focus on what the General was saying and not worry about Brian.

Almost impossible to do.

"The Dogs have broken through once again," the general said. "It seems our destroying their base sort of made them angry."

"What?" Dot asked, stunned. The other captains all shifted and shook their heads in understanding.

The general went on. "They broke through our outer defenses yesterday Earth time. We've had a few skirmishes with them along the border over the last few days, but this breakthrough now is major. Our allies in the *League* and border patrols couldn't stop them and had to pull back."

"That bad, huh?" Dot asked. A feeling of dread was quickly replacing the wonderful feel of being young again.

The general nodded. "This morning we got data that make it clear that they are headed to Earth to destroy the center of the *League* once and for all. And they have enough ships to do it."

Dot stepped forward toward the big screen and looked intently at the general, not letting the worry filling her chest show. Since without Brian here, she was the most senior captain in the group. She felt it was her job to ask the questions.

"How many ships did they send?"

"Over five hundred of their warships got through the border and are headed for your position at a very slow, but still Trans-Galactic speed," the general said. "Your job is to try to slow them down even more, give us time behind you to form a second and third line of defense to turn them and keep them from reaching Earth."

"Understood," Dot said.

"Anyone have any questions?" the general asked

Dot glanced at the other captains.

All looked firm and determined. But none of the captains seemed to want to say anything.

She turned back to the general. "We'll slow them down. Maybe knock their numbers down a few. You can count on that."

The general nodded. "I knew I could depend on all of you."

The screen went blank.

She took a deep breath, stunned. At least the general had the common decency to not say that it had been nice knowing them all. Or even good luck.

This would be the last mission for all of them.

The general knew it. They all knew it.

This was their funeral.

She would not make it back to see Brian again.

That thought just broke her heart and she shuddered.

She would die young and in deep space, just as Brian had always hoped he would. Better than in his sleep in the nursing home back on Earth. So that meant that if he wasn't going to die there, she had to win this coming battle somehow.

She took a deep breath, shoved the fear aside, and turned to the other captains. "Looks like we've got some work ahead of us."

She strolled for the door, headed for her Command Center.

If this was her last mission and she would never see Brian again, she intended to make it a good one.

If she had anything to say about it, she was going to save Earth one last time.

And the man she loved in the process.

TWENTY-FOUR

April 20th, 1962
Equivalent Earth Time
Location: Deep Space

"SO, HOW WAS the dreamboat Acting Captain Knudson?" Carrie asked as Dot entered *The Blooming Rose* command center. "Steve here can't seem to concentrate."

"You know I'm here, don't you?" Steve said.

"Ignoring you like usual," Carrie said, staring at Dot. "You look upset, Captain. Was it that bad?"

"This mission sucks."

She dropped down into her command chair and just stared at the screen showing the empty space around them and the other seven *EPL* warships.

"So what do they have us doing this time?" Steve asked. "Can't be much worse than those reptile things we had to clean up on Darren Six last mission."

"The Dogs got pissed at us for sending a moon at their military base

117

and broke out of their fence," Dot said. "We're supposed to try to slow them down until the *League* can mount a decent defense behind us."

"Crap," Steve said.

"You're kidding, right?" Carrie asked.

Dot didn't turn to look at her second-in-command. She knew that Carrie's face would be white.

"How many?" Steve asked, his voice low and hushed.

"Five hundred of their warships. Eight of us."

"Oh, for a moment there I thought we were in trouble," Steve said.

"Does the League have any idea how we're supposed to do this?" Carrie asked.

"Not a word," Dot said, smiling at her friend. "They left it up to our ancient wisdom to come up with something to slow them down."

"I hate it when they do that," Steve said.

"Yeah, me too," Dot said, trying not to laugh. Thank God for friends around her. They always made things easier in the toughest situations.

"You two work on finding out how much time we have until they get here, what speed they're moving, so on, and I'll brief the rest of the crew. Call them all to the rec room, would you, Steve?"

She pushed herself easily to her feet and headed out.

She could have done this task from her command chair, but she wanted to feel young again, walk quickly again, just one more time.

And besides, her crew deserved to learn they were about to die from her personally.

It was the least she could do.

It was halfway through the personnel briefing with the almost forty members of his gathered crew that Dot came up with the plan that just might give them a little better chance of staying alive a little longer.

And maybe in the long run, save Earth.

A few minutes later she finished the briefing and sprinted back to the Command Center of the ship, her shoes making almost no sound on the rubber floors of the hallways

She enjoyed the run, but then finally dropped into her chair. Wow, she loved being young, being in shape, being able to just walk. Let alone run.

"How long?"

"Five hundred Dog Warships will be barking on our front steps in exactly thirty-five minutes," Carrie said.

"Perfect," Dot said.

"Perfect?" Steve asked. "You have a very weird way of looking at this situation."

Dot laughed. "Steve, contact all the other ships and have them be ready to match the Dog's Trans-Galactic speed in fifteen minutes."

Steve glanced over at her. "You really like getting your butt kicked by slug-looking poodles, don't you?"

"How old are you, Steve?" Dot asked, her fingers working on the board as she talked.

"Six months short of the big eighty-five," Steve said. "And still getting around just fine with the ladies at the home I might add."

"They can't be very picky," Carrie said.

"And how long did it take us to get from Earth to this position?" Dot asked.

"From what measuring point?" Steve asked.

Dot liked Steve because he understood all the crazy things that went on with space and time on these ships.

"Earth time?" Dot asked.

"Over sixty or so years," Steve said.

"Transport shipboard time? How long did the trip take to get us out here?"

"Six days, ten hours, and a few odd minutes while we slept like babies."

"And it will take us that long to get back?" Dot asked, "Right?"

"Shipboard time," Steve said. "They'll speed up the ship slightly on the return voyage and we'll end up back in our beds less than thirty minutes after we left, Earth time that is, even if we spend weeks out here. You know that."

Dot nodded. It was why she knew she could safely leave Brian sleeping. She was only going to be gone for a few minutes in Brian's time if she survived.

"So how are the Dogs handling the same matter/relativity/time problem on their flight toward Earth at the speeds they are traveling?"

"How the hell would I—"

Suddenly Steve stopped and smiled at Dot. "I see where you're headed Captain. Their life spans are shorter than ours, right?"

"Exactly," Dot said. "Which is why they are moving at a slow Trans-Galactic speed, because they don't dare go any faster or they would end up Dog-pups or not exist at all when they reached Earth."

"Which means they have to be damn old Dogs right now," Steve said, "at the beginning of their flight. They cleared out their Dog nursing homes and have them flying the ships."

"Exactly," Dot said. "And you and I both know how well old Dogs like us move back on Earth."

Steve laughed. "We're young and right now they're old. Really, really old. You're right! Perfect!"

"You know, I think you two are right," Carrie said, shaking her head.

"Scary, huh?" Steve said, smiling.

"Every so often we get one," Dot said, grinning at her second-in-command.

Then Dot turned back to her controls. "I'd say it's time to kick some wrinkled Dog butt, don't you?"

She punched the communications link to the seven captains of the other *League* ships. Quickly, she explained what she had figured out and how they were going to fight the Dogs.

"Launch all single men fighters on my command when we reach attack positions," she said to the captains. Each warship carried a fleet of thirty single fighters.

"Have your pilots keep the single-man fighters on full thrust and constantly turning, diving, retreating," Dot said to the other Captains. "Break the fighters into units of ten with each ten ship unit attacking one dog ship, then moving on. Have them keep moving as fast as they can all the time. The aliens flying those ships are slow and old right now, just as we all were when they brought us out here. Remember that and maybe we can buy the *League* some real time."

All the captains agreed and with a wish of good luck, they all signed off.

Twenty minutes later they launched the single-man fighters.

And a few minutes later the Dog warships appeared on the view screens.

They were ugly, sausage-looking ships, with slick-looking hulls and protruding weapons systems and thrusters. The fighters had been ordered to stay away from in front of the weapons and target the thrusters. Their mission was to slow them down and, as Steve had said, there was no better way to do that than shoot a Dog warship in the ass.

TWENTY-FIVE

April 20th, 1962
Equivalent Earth Time
Location: Deep Space

THERE WAS SOMETHING about the formation of Dog warships that bothered Dot, but for the few minutes it took to get her fighters staged around the alien fleet, she couldn't figure it out.

Around her Carrie and Steve were busy keeping *The Blooming Rose* out of reach of the Dogs long-range weapons for a moment. After the fighters had their fun, then it would be time for the big warships to take a run at them.

So she had a moment to just sit and watch the fight, not something she normally liked doing. She had always been much more of a person who waded in and took the lead. But for the moment, the small fighters needed the room to flit around like fleas.

She stared at the formation of the Dog fleet. With their weird long shapes, there was just something about them she couldn't get a handle on.

Then suddenly it struck her.

They were staggered like bowling pins on an alley, with lead ships protecting other ships in the middle of the formation.

The Dog fleet was flying in bowling pin formations, a couple dozen of them per formation.

She and her husband had spent a lot of years bowling with friends a couple times a week until all their families started to get too old and his job kept him too busy. She had loved to bowl.

Not as much as she loved to dance, but since the accident that killed him and crippled her, she hadn't thought of bowling at all, where every night she had dreamed of dancing until Brian got her out here in space and allowed her to be young and dance for real again.

She had loved the smell of the old bowling alley in Chicago she and her husband used to go to, the feel of the silly leather shoes they had to wear, the weight of the ball in her hands. She usually came close to beating her husband most nights, and would have if he wasn't as competitive as she was and a darned fine athlete.

She loved most of all the feeling of getting a strike, sending that big ball right down the center of the pins.

She stared at the Dog ships and understood how they might just make a difference in this fight. It might get them all killed a little faster, but if her idea worked, it would cause huge damage to the Dog fleet.

"You know how to override the Trans-Galactic drive limitations on this ship?" Dot asked, turning to Carrie as the fighters broke into attack groups and swarmed around the oncoming Dog warships like so many bugs on a hot summer's afternoon.

"I think I could do it," Carrie said, frowning and looking at Dot. "Why?"

"I'm just wondering," Dot said. "Tell me what would happen if we plowed right through the middle of that fleet at full Trans-Galactic speed?"

"Besides destroy us?" Carrie said.

"I'm not so sure it would hurt us that bad," Dot said. "If I remember right, at full and complete Trans-Galactic speed, we're on complete force-field shields, big enough to knock just about anything short of a small moon out of the way. I think I'm remembering right from all those confusing lectures back in basic training."

"Actually, our shields would just knock a small hole through a moon," Steve said. "Like drilling from one side to the other."

Carrie stared at Dot for a moment, then glanced back at the big view screen showing the alien fleet.

"They sort of do look like bowling pins, don't they?" Dot asked.

"Bowling for Dogs," Steve said, clapping. "I love it! I haven't been bowling for years."

Carrie set to work to see if she could get complete control of the top speed of the Trans-Galactic drive controls. If anyone in the fleet could do it, Carrie could. In the Command Center they had control over slower Trans-Galactic speeds for short trips and battles like this one, but never full speed. It was just too dangerous to leave in the hands of a bunch of senior citizens, no matter how well-trained.

In thirty seconds, Carrie looked up, smiling. "Got it. Easier than I thought."

On the screen the fighters were having some luck. The Dog warships were firing, but not really hitting anything. The fighters were picking at the thrusters of the ships like a kid picked at a scab.

Two dog ships were already dead in space, left behind by the fleet. But there were already four single-man fighters destroyed, four elderly humans who wouldn't be returning alive to their nursing home rooms tonight on Earth.

In fact, the way those fighters had exploded, replacement bodies would have to be put in those beds to fool the families.

Dot quickly called the other captains and explained her idea, looking for any of them to knock a hole in the idea.

None did.

For a moment they all looked sort of shocked at the idea.

After that, they all just broke into smiles and a couple made really bad bowling jokes.

"Have the fighters pull back and give us plenty of room. We'll give it a shot. Keep them back for five minutes or until you hear from me again," Dot said. "We hope to be coming back the same way."

All acting captains wished her luck and signed off.

"Yup, Acting Captain Knudson is good enough to eat," Carrie said, smiling at Steve. "Five course meal and three desserts."

"Yeah, I do a mean barbeque," Steve said.

"Sloppy and covered in sauce," Carrie said. "Figures."

"When you are ready," Dot said to her first officer as she shook her head.

"Not too far," Steve said.

"I'll be careful," Carrie said, smiling at Steve. "Last thing I want is to have to change your diapers."

Dot, on instructions from Carrie, carefully sat the Trans-Galactic drive for only a six second burst. That would take them through the Dog Warship fleet and some distance beyond, but not too far. Too far and they might end up too young to pilot the ship back into position. Or worse, end up in Dog territory beyond the border.

Then Dot moved *The Blooming Rose* around and to a position a distance in front of the Dog fleet.

"Ready to lose a little age and wrinkles?" Dot asked.

"And with luck, a few Dog Warships in the process," Steve said.

"Right down the lane," Carrie said. "Go for the strike."

Dot punched the T-G Drive engage, and for the first time in all the missions, she saw what space looked like at full Trans-Galactic speed.

It was a blur of black and white streaks.

Nothing more.

Not even pretty.

Just weird.

She was glad she normally slept through it.

Then as quickly as it started, it ended and the stars were back, solid in space.

There was no sign of the Dog Warships, or the rest of the *League* fleet.

"Damage report?" Dot asked.

"Nothing major," Steve said as his fingers flew over his board, checking everything.

"Some really minor strain on the shields, but they are holding fine at ninety-eight percent," Carrie said.

"Where are we?" Dot asked.

"We've gone a bunch closer to the Dog Border and we're four weeks younger than a few seconds ago," Carrie said.

"I knew I felt better," Dot said. "Don't you just love how this relativity and mass and time stuff works?"

"Yeah," Steve said. "Just wish I really understood it."

"I hear you there," Dot said.

"Thank heavens one of us on this ship does," Carrie said, laughing.

Dot didn't argue with that at all.

Dot flipped the ship over and, with a quick run of her fingers over the board, reset the controls to return them to just a few seconds after they had left and just a slight distance farther ahead of the Dog fleet to make up for the speed of the Dog ships.

"Getting older," Dot said.

Again the view screens showed black and white streaks for a long six seconds, then normal space returned.

"Damage?" Dot asked.

"No more than last time," Carrie said. "Shields at ninety-seven percent."

"Holy cow!" Steve said. "I think we got a strike."

"Maybe two," Dot said, staring at the damage they had done to the Dogs. They had punched not just one, but two holes in the fleet of Dog warships, damaging and destroying at least thirty of them in the process.

And the single-man fighters were now swooping in to take advantage of the confusion to cause even more damage.

For the first time since Dot heard about the mission, she felt there might be a chance she would see Brian again.

Just a chance.

But there was a lot of work to do.

"Get ready to hit them again," Dot said. "Tell the fighters to get out of the way in thirty seconds. We're coming through."

As they waited the few seconds for the fighters to again withdraw, Steve said, "They're going to come up with a terrible name for this, you know."

"And what would that be?" Dot asked

"The Leeds' Yo-Yo Maneuver," Steve said.

"Sounds good to me," Dot said, laughing.

"Nah," Carrie said. "I think it will be the Leeds' Bowling Maneuver."

Dot waited until the other pilots confirmed that they were ready and the fighters were out of the way, then she punched them back into full Trans-Galactic speed once again, aiming directly at the thickest part of the Dog fleet.

And for a few seconds, she got even younger.

And she really, really loved being young.

She just needed the man she loved here beside her to make this perfect.

TWENTY-SIX

April 20th, 1962
Equivalent Earth Time
Location: Deep Space

AFTER EVERYTHING WAS cleaned up, and she had sent Carrie and Steve to get some dinner and enjoy the coming party, Dot put in a call to General Banks.

"Captain Leeds," the general said, nodding as he came on the screen. His face was again smiling, the wrinkles that surrounded his eyes and mouth clear once again. "Great job out there."

"Thank you, General," she said. "But I'm worried about Captain Saber."

He nodded and his expression became serious. "We are watching his condition very closely. If you hadn't been able to stop the Dogs, we would have taken a chance and pulled him to lead a second line of defense."

Dot nodded. That made sense to her. If they could let him rest, they would, but if they couldn't, why not have the best Captain in the fleet fighting a second line of defense for Earth, even if it endangered his life.

"So if his condition worsens, what are you going to do?"

"Captain," the General said, his voice firm, his eyes intent. "We have our procedures and our rules and all of us are bound by them, including Captain Saber."

She started to say something, but he held up his hand. "I have been told Captain Saber is stronger. We are watching his condition. Again, great job today."

With that he clicked off, leaving the screen blank in front of her.

Somehow she managed to not put her fist through the blank screen.

Then she almost called him back, but decided that until she got back and understood what was really going on with Brian, she didn't dare. She might have just saved all of Earth, but it didn't seem that the *EPL* was going to be very grateful with the man she loved.

The man who had saved them all many more times than she had.

She didn't dance that night at the party, but instead just sat and drank and watched Acting Captain Marian Knudson and Dot's third-in-command, Steve, flirt. They were clearly good together.

And Steve made Marian laugh, which from what Brian had told Dot, was unusual.

Dot wondered how many people had watched her and Brian do the same thing over the last few years.

Finally, it was time to head back.

Normally she hated going in and putting on her old nightgown and going back to her old body. But this time she was anxious to be old again.

Brian was there.

And spending even another minute without him wasn't something she really wanted to do.

She crawled into her sleep coffin and closed the lid, letting the gas knock her out.

A moment later she was being picked up from the coffin by Lieutenant Sherri.

"Good mission, Captain?" the Lieutenant asked.

"We got the job done," Dot said.

What seemed like only a moment later she was being carried through the chill evening air of Chicago and into Brian's room.

He still seemed to be sleeping comfortably.

The lieutenant carried Dot across the hallway and put her in her wheelchair as Dot instructed.

"Have a good night, Captain," Lieutenant Sherri said, snapping off a salute and heading back across the hall and out the door.

Dot waited a moment, then wheeled her chair across the hallway and into Brian's room.

She reached up and touched his arm and he stirred slightly, but kept sleeping.

She moved in close to his bed, locked the brakes on her chair, and put her head down on his bed next to him.

Somehow, she had to save him.

She could save all of Earth.

Why couldn't she save the man she loved?

TWENTY-SEVEN

April 20th, 2022
Actual Earth Time
Location: Chicago

AN HOUR LATER Joyce, the night nurse, woke her and helped her
across the hallway and into her own bed. She didn't think she would be
able to sleep because she was so worried, but she did, waking at her
normal time.

After her morning bath and dressing, she pushed her wheelchair
ahead of her out into the hallway, working to get her old legs loosened
up a little. She had to see how Brian was doing, then get a little breakfast and come back to sit with him.

Two people she didn't recognize were talking in whispers in the
hallway and Brian's door was closed. One was a middle-aged man, the
other a younger woman. Both had on dark winter coats and jeans. The
woman had dark brown hair pulled back and stuffed in the collar of
her coat.

The man was tall and held himself with great posture, his thinning brown hair combed back and slightly long. The younger woman looked like she might be his daughter.

"Is Brian all right?" Dot asked, her stomach twisting into a hard knot as she moved toward them and Brian's door.

He couldn't have died in the middle of the night. He just couldn't have.

"We're not sure," the middle-aged man said, stepping away from the young girl with a nod.

The girl smiled at Dot and then turned and headed for the nurse's station down the hall.

The man stuck out his hand and smiled. "I'm Brian Wilson Saber, Brian's oldest son. But I have always gone by Wilson. And yes, my dad loved the Beach Boys. You must be Dot Leeds."

"I am," she said, shaking Wilson's hand.

Now that he said it, she could see the clear likeness. She only knew Brian young or old. Not middle-aged, which is why she hadn't seen the resemblance with his son instantly.

But he was clearly as handsome as his father. Brian had talked about Wilson at times and told her that someday he would make a great Captain.

"Nice meeting you," Wilson said, shaking her hand gently and then releasing it. "Dad has talked a lot about you."

"I hope all good," she said, smiling.

"All very good," he said, smiling back with Brian's smile.

"So what do you mean you're not sure how Brian is?" she asked.

"My daughter has headed to the lunchroom to get something to eat," Wilson said. "How about we go there and you can have some breakfast and I'll try to explain what the doctors have said."

She nodded. At least Brian's son was willing to help her and get her into the loop. That was a start. She would have to be very careful to not say anything to him about the *EPL*. Even though Brian had said Wilson would be a good Captain some day, he hadn't told her that he knew about the *EPL*. And he didn't need to know that she hoped to save his father by getting him out of here somehow and into deep space.

To Brian's son, that would not be saving him, since his father would be considered dead at that point.

But Dot had no other choice. She had to save the man she loved by killing him in his son's eyes.

Wilson walked with her slowly down the hall and into the lunch-room. Again the bright room smelled of pancakes and eggs. The drapes were all open showing the bright Chicago spring morning outside the windows. She had always loved Chicago in the spring, especially after a hard winter. It always felt like a rebirth.

After she met Brian's granddaughter, a young woman named Sue who worked as a head nurse at another nursing home about ten miles away, Dot steered the conversation back to Brian.

Neither one of them let on that they knew about the *EPL*, so she was careful.

Wilson looked worried, an expression she had seen on his father's face many times.

"The doctor thinks Dad may have had another small stroke yester-day," Wilson said. "He wants Dad to rest and his condition is now being monitored every few hours by the nurses here."

Dot took a deep breath and let it out slowly. "That doesn't sound good, does it?"

"We honestly don't know," Wilson said and his daughter nodded. Brian's granddaughter clearly had some medical knowledge as a nurse and that was who Dot would turn to.

"Any idea how long?" Dot asked Sue after they paused for their breakfasts to be delivered. Dot had her normal eggs and pancakes and both Wilson and his daughter had a glass of orange juice and toast.

"He might get a little stronger and last for another two or three years," Sue said. "The kind of small strokes he suffers are that way. We just have to see what is happening with him, and if he gains strength in the next day or so."

133

So that was what the brass in charge of the *Earth Protection League* were hoping. They wanted their top front-line fighter to get better here and keep going on missions for them.

But if he didn't, that's what worried Dot. She had no idea if the *League* would just let him die at that point.

"I'll watch him as much as I'm able," Dot said.

"Thank you," Wilson said. "I know dad would appreciate that."

Dot nodded and tried to force herself to eat. If she was going to sit with Brian, she needed to keep her strength up.

That last thing either of them needed was for her to get sick as well.

TWENTY-EIGHT

April 23rd, 2022
Actual Earth Time
Location: Chicago

THE LAST TWO days had been a total nightmare for Dot. She had spent her day either resting beside Brian or eating the three meals she didn't want to eat or even taste.

Both Wilson and Sue stopped in at least twice a day and often sat with Brian as well. Dot had talked to them, but no one else.

Sue was getting worried that Brian wasn't getting better. He hadn't really even woken up in the last two days other than to moan and shift slightly. He seemed to be stuck and sometimes his breathing got so raspy, Dot wasn't sure if he was going to make it for another ten minutes.

If Sue, who was a full nurse, was worried, that just terrified Dot.

She hoped that in some way the *League* was watching. But she wasn't sure how they could be. No one talked to her at all.

Dot was starting to become convinced they were just going to let Brian die.

By the morning of the third day, she was emotionally drained, and getting more tired by the hour.

At one point, she fell asleep sitting in her chair with her head on Brian's bed beside him, and she dreamed once again of dancing.

Since she had learned of the *League* and Brian had danced with her, the dreams of dancing, of being free, hadn't come back.

She wasn't sure what that meant.

But now they were back.

Finally, on the morning of the third day, Brian woke up.

She had just returned from breakfast and sitting next to Brian's bed in her wheelchair. Wilson was reading a magazine in another chair he had pulled in from somewhere.

Other than to nod hello, they hadn't talked.

Brian moaned and opened his eyes.

Then he looked at Dot and smiled.

But it wasn't the vibrant smile of the man she loved, but instead the smile of a man saying goodbye.

She jumped to her feet and leaned forward in case he wanted to try to talk.

He tried to whisper, but clearly his throat was dry.

She quickly got him an ice chip from the cup of ice she kept near his head and gave it to him to wet his lips.

Wilson was standing behind her, watching.

Brian smiled and nodded, then said, "I see you two have finally met."

"She's as wonderful as you said, Dad," Wilson said.

Brian smiled weakly. "I know."

Then Brian tried to say something more, but it came out only a whisper.

She leaned down to hear him better.

"Marry me," he said. "Please. I want to go dancing."

"Of course," she said.

He sighed and said, "Good."

Then he closed his eyes and for a moment Dot thought he was gone.

Finally, his rough breathing resumed, but barely.

Dot stood upright, holding for balance onto the thin arm of the man she loved, listening to him struggle for breath. She couldn't believe what he had just asked.

They had talked about spending their lives together, but never about marriage. Why now?

There was something she was missing.

"What did he say?" Wilson asked.

Dot looked up at Wilson and shook her head. "He asked me to marry him."

Wilson nodded and said nothing. He pulled out his phone and called Sue and asked her to come over as soon as she could.

Dot sat down in her wheelchair and stared at Brian lying there in that bed, almost dead.

He was the smartest man she had ever known. Why had he waited until this moment to ask her to marry him?

What in the world was he up to?

TWENTY-NINE

April 24th, 2022
Actual Earth Time
Location: Chicago

SHE SAT WITH Brian for another half hour, then decided she couldn't take it anymore. She had to do something and do it now.

Time really was running out.

Sue had gotten there a few minutes before and looking very worried. At one point Wilson had tucked the blankets around his father and told him to hang on.

Sue had taken out a stethoscope and listened to Brian's heart, then shook her head. "Not much longer."

There didn't seem to be anything they could do, or any doctor here on Earth could do. Brian's old body was just taking his final breaths.

Dot just couldn't let Brian die.

Not like this.

Not after all the times he had saved Earth.

This wasn't right or fair.

"I'll be right back," she said to Wilson and Sue.

Then taking her wheelchair, she walked behind it, pushing it ahead of her out of Brian's room and down the hall toward the nurse's station. Brian's meaning was clear as far as she was concerned. He wanted her to marry him and live in space. If she had anything to say about it, that was what she planned on doing.

She was going to get him out of here and back to his young body somehow.

She didn't know how, but she wasn't going to let him die without trying something.

It was the least the *EPL* could do. She just needed to point that out to a few generals, maybe at the top of her lungs.

The clock above the wall behind the nurse's station said it was only a few minutes after eleven in the morning.

The nurse on duty was a woman by the name of Joyce. She sometimes worked days, other times she worked nights. Joyce was often the one on duty when they went on missions. That was enough.

Joyce had a large smile, graying dark hair that was pulled back and tied, and bright green eyes. She looked middle-aged and wore a bright gold wedding ring. Joyce had always been nice and kind to Dot, something Dot appreciated.

Dot waited a moment until there was no one else within listening range, then leaned on the counter and said clearly to Joyce.

"Brian isn't going to make it through the day. I want to talk to one of the generals with the *EPL* and I won't take no for an answer."

Joyce looked stunned for a moment. Actually, more than stunned. Shocked.

Dot expected her to ask what exactly Dot was talking about, but instead Joyce looked in both directions to make sure no one was listening.

"General Brooks is aware of the situation with Captain Saber."

"Then tell him to get his ass on the phone to me in ten minutes,"

Dot said, her old voice taking on her captain traits and power. "I'll be in my room."

"Yes, Captain," Joyce said, nodding, a look of worry crossing her face.

That was the first time in four years anyone at Shady Valley Nursing Home had referred to her by her *League* rank.

"Tell the general to make it snappy," Dot said and turned, pushing her wheelchair ahead of her back down the hall toward her room, doing her best to keep her back straight and her walk steady.

The greatest captain in the long history of the *Earth Protection League* wasn't going to die today if she had anything to say about it.

And she planned on having a lot to say.

THIRTY

April 24th, 2022
Actual Earth Time
Location: Chicago

BY THE TIME she got to her room, she had something figured out. Brian had asked her to marry him because he knew that was important in getting them off the planet.

It was the only reason for his timing like that. He knew something she didn't.

It wasn't a dying wish or a hope of a man wanting to not die.

Brian knew he was dying, and he knew that if they weren't getting married, the regulations wouldn't allow him to leave. Or some such stupid organizational rule like that.

That had to be the reason.

Dot made it to her room, pushed the door closed, and had just sat in her chair when her desk phone rang. It sounded odd to her ears, it seldom rang since her son wasn't much of a caller.

She took a deep breath and picked up the phone. Then, without so much as a hello, she said, "You have many bases out near the borders where humans from here are living and working and raising families. Correct?"

"That is correct," General Brooks said, his voice clearly hesitant.

"Including Steven's Base," she said, remembering where she and Brian had danced and spent two wonderful days just last week after saving Earth from a large moon.

"Yes," General Brooks said.

"Captain Saber's conditioned has worsened this morning," Dot said.

"We are aware of the captain's condition," General Brooks said.

"Are you aware," Dot said, making her voice very firm, "that Captain Saber asked me to marry him and I said yes."

There was a silence on the other end of the line. It was as if they had been disconnected, but it was clear they had not.

Dot waited for a moment, then went on, deciding to push the point.

"We want to start a family and keep working for the *League*," she said firmly. "I am assuming that is a condition to immigrating to that area of space."

She was taking a chance at that, because she didn't know for sure, but it again would make sense considering Brian's proposal of marriage. It hadn't been romantic, but it had given her some great ammunition to use to save his life.

"It is," General Brooks said after a moment. "Intent to start a family is required to settle in that area of space permanently."

Dot shook her head. Why hadn't she and Brian talked about this more, got this done long before now? Both of them were just so damned old-fashioned for their own good at times.

"We're planning on have a brood," she said, even though they had never really talked about having children. "A whole mess of little Sabers running around messing things up. Now get us the hell out of here before my future husband dies."

Again there was silence on the other end for a moment.

Then General Brooks said, "It's not that simple."

Dot barely kept herself from yelling. "Neither was saving this stupid planet a dozen times, including from that moon last week and all those Dog Warships three days ago. But Captain Saber and I have done just that for you. So with respect, General, I don't give a damn about simple. Get my future husband out of her. Alive. And do it quickly."

"Think this through," Captain," General Brooks said. "You will lose your family."

"You know my son lives on the West Coast and you know we are not close? Correct?" she asked.

"I know of your family," General Brooks said.

"I have said goodbye to my family a number of times over the years," Dot said. "Captain Saber is my family now. And I sure as hell don't want to lose him."

"I understand," General Brooks said.

"So get Captain Saber out of here now, give me a couple days to wrap up things here before I join him."

There was silence on the other end, so Dot kept pushing.

"Captain Saber and I are good breeding stock for your colony, wouldn't you say?"

"You're sure about this?" General Brooks asked one more time.

"I'm sure," she said. "But if you don't hurry, the option will be gone. He may go at any moment."

"That bad?" the General asked, clearly finally starting to understand what Dot had been saying all along. There was actual worry in that question.

"That bad," Dot said. "Why do you think I demanded this call now?"

Again there was silence for a moment.

"Thirty minutes," General Brooks said. "Work with the nurse to keep people away from his room. Get his sliding glass door open."

"How long will it take?" she asked.

"Five minutes to switch him out," General Brooks said.

"Done," Dot said.

And the line went dead.

Dot hung up the phone and took a deep breath before standing and heading for the door to her room and the nurse's station, pushing her wheelchair as quickly as she could in front of her.

Now if Brian could just hang on long enough to be rescued from old age.

THIRTY-ONE

April 24th, 2022
Actual Earth Time
Location: Chicago

AS DOT APPROACHED the nurse's station, Joyce hung up the phone and nodded at her.

Dot suddenly felt like she was a spy in a cold war movie.

"I'll go in and get his door unlocked," Dot said. "His son and grand-daughter are in there as well, so I'll ask to talk with them in the hall."

Joyce started to say something, but her phone rang.

Dot watched as Joyce listened for a moment, then hung up.

"They will be coming through Captain Saber's door in exactly ten minutes."

Dot glanced at the big clock on the wall. It was exactly twenty-one minutes after eleven. She turned back for Brian's room.

Joyce took a moment before she could get out from behind the nurse's station, so Dot almost beat her to Brian's room. Joyce held Brian's door open for her.

Inside the room, it took a moment for Dot's eyes to adjust to the dimness as the hallway door swung closed. Under the sheet and light blanket, she could see Brian was still breathing.

Oh, thank heavens. He still had a chance.

Joyce went right to him and checked his heartbeat quickly, then looked under one eyelid.

She shook her head. Dot wasn't sure what that meant, but it clearly wasn't good.

Sue stepped up beside Joyce. "Not long?"

"Very close," Joyce said. "They are coming."

"Goodbye, Grandpa," Sue said, leaning over and kissing her grandfather on the cheek.

Dot headed for the sliding door into the center court to unlatch it, but Wilson stood and said simply, "I'll get it, Captain."

He unlocked the sliding door, but didn't open it.

Then he turned and saluted Dot.

"I suppose it's time I introduce myself to my future step-mother. Commander Wilson Saber at your service, Captain. I assume dad never said anything about his entire family being involved in the *EPL*."

Dot stood there, her mouth open, not sure what to say.

She looked at Sue, then back at Wilson. Both Brian's son and granddaughter were part of the *League*. Why hadn't Brian said something about that to her.

"Typical of him," Wilson said, shaking his head.

"Thank heavens you convinced them into doing a daylight extraction," Sue said to Dot. "I don't think he would have made it to later tonight as planned."

"I'm sure he wouldn't have," Joyce said.

"Yes, thank-you, Captain," Wilson said. "For saving my father's life."

"Joyce and I'll be outside guarding the door," Sue said, patting Dot's shoulder as she went past. "Thank you for saving my grandfather. And keep him alive until I can get out there, would you?"

There wasn't a thing Dot could say, so all she did was nod. She was too shocked at the moment to say anything.

And relieved that they were coming for Brian.

As the door to the hallway closed, the exterior door slid open and two men carrying a stretcher came in, followed by two others carrying another stretcher with a body on it.

One of the first men saluted Dot and Wilson, then went to the bed and quickly checked Brian.

"We got to move now," he said after a moment, his voice urgent, but in control.

The two quickly got Brian on the stretcher and as they did, Brian opened his eyes.

"Hang in there, dad," Wilson said. "I'll catch up with you in twenty years or so along the way."

Brian smiled.

"Try not to get yourself killed before I get out there," Wilson said.

"I don't think Captain Leeds is going to let that happen," Brian whispered, just loud enough for her and Wilson to hear.

Dot almost broke into tears right there. Just hearing him talk again was wonderful.

Then Brian closed his eyes and the two men rushed him out the door, vanishing almost as soon as they cleared the edge of the room.

The other two men quickly placed the other body on the bed. It looked exactly like Brian, right down to the old nightshirt stained with food. But this body was very, very dead.

They both nodded to Dot and Wilson and then stepped outside, vanishing almost instantly as they cleared the door.

Wilson went over and pulled the sliding glass door closed and made sure the drapes were in place to keep the room dim.

Dot stared at the dead husk on the bed. It looked like the old Brian, but she knew it wasn't.

Then she turned to Wilson who was also staring at the body under the sheet on the bed. "You and the *League* had no intention of letting him die, did you?"

Wilson shook his head. "They were going to make an exception to the marriage policy for him. But it seems they didn't need to."

"You planned on taking him out tonight?"

Wilson nodded. "I don't think he would have made it. Thank you again for pushing the general and saving Dad's life."

"Let's hope he survived," Dot said. "From my understanding, it sometimes takes time to get those transport ships going."

"They'll save him," Wilson said. "They'll just put him on a warship and jump him a few years if it's coming down to that, before putting him on a transport."

She nodded. "Of course."

"Just wish I could make the wedding," Wilson said. "But someone would have to change my diapers if I tried it."

"We'll send you pictures," Dot said, laughing for the first time in days and days. And that felt wonderful.

More wonderful than she wanted to admit right now.

Wilson smiled back, then looked at the body on the bed. "Guess I have some phone calls to make and a funeral to attend. Makes it a lot easier knowing he's going to be out there alive, and with you."

Dot touched Wilson's arm and then pushed her chair out of the room as Wilson held the door for her.

Joyce and Sue were standing in the hallway watching them come out.

"They got him away," Wilson said.

Both Joyce and Sue nodded.

At that moment, Sue's cell phone rang.

She looked annoyed, but glanced at it and then answered it.

After a long moment of listening, she said simply, "Thank you, General. I'll pass the word."

She looked at the other three. "He made it, but barely. They jumped him a few years away to make sure and then put him on a larger transport to Davis Station."

Dot felt her knees get weak, but Wilson slipped a hand under her arm and steadied her as she held the handles on her wheelchair.

Sue smiled at Dot. "The general had a message for you. He said to tell you that Captain Saber will be waiting for you on Steven's Base. It seems you have a wedding to plan and some dancing to do."

At that, Dot simply moved around her wheelchair and sat down.

PART FIVE
ONE LAST TRIP OUT

FOUR NIGHTS LATER

THIRTY-TWO

April 28th, 2022
Actual Earth Time
Location: Chicago

IT SURPRISED DOT that she had so few "affairs" she had to wrap up. After living in assisted care for over twenty years, she didn't have much, and the insurance money from the settlement from the car accident, that had killed her first husband and crippled her, would go to her son in her will. She had spent very, very little of it over the years. That money would make his life easier, and she had put some of it in trusts for her grandchildren's college education.

There just hadn't been much for her to to spend money on considering she was crippled and her living in Shady Valley was paid for in the settlement.

The worst part of getting everything in order had come with the phone call to her son and two grandkids. She really couldn't say goodbye, but she sort of did anyway. She would miss them, even though she seldom saw them.

She hoped they would miss her, even though the grandkids didn't really know her at all. They had lived so far away for so long, and there had been so few visits.

Shady Valley Nursing Home had a small memorial service for Brian, but Dot had claimed she wasn't feeling well and had skipped it. She just didn't feel much like mourning the man she would be marrying very shortly.

That just seemed wrong in so many ways.

And she really didn't know anyone else who lived here, since she had spent all her time with Brian over the years, especially the last four.

It would have been another matter if he hadn't made it out in time.

A totally different matter, actually.

She didn't want to let herself think about that at all. He had made it and was young and waiting for her. That was all that mattered.

So finally, on the fourth morning after Brian left, when Lieutenant Sherri came to wake her up at a little after three in the morning, Dot was ready to go.

And she surprisingly had no regrets.

All she could see was a bright and happy future ahead.

"I hear congratulations are in order," Lieutenant Sherri said, smiling as she helped Dot out of her bed and made sure her wheelchair was there and sturdy to hold onto.

"I guess so," Dot said. "I understand I have a fiancé waiting for me at Steven's Base. Seems we have a wedding to plan."

"I hear it's beautiful there," the lieutenant said as they started for the doorway to the hallway, Dot holding onto the lieutenant's arm and walking slowly to let her old legs get going again.

In the hallway Joyce was standing there, smiling. "I'll miss you, Captain."

Dot indicated that Joyce should give her a hug.

The nurse did.

"Thank you for your help in saving Brian," Dot said, smiling at Joyce.

"You are more than welcome," Joyce said. "And I hope to be out your way in about thirty more years or so."

Dot laughed. "You'll be young and I'll be middle-aged by that point. Sometimes this is just very strange."

Joyce laughed.

"I'll be about twenty years behind her," Lieutenant Sherri said.

And all three of them laughed at how they would all be back in their same ages they were now by that point.

"Look us up," Dot said, marveling at the fact that when Lieutenant Sherri got out there, Dot and Brian would be old again and the lieutenant would look just as she did now. But fifty years will have passed.

With one last wave to Joyce, Dot and Lieutenant Sherri moved slowly into Brian's empty room. It had been cleaned and was waiting for the next resident.

Dot wondered if that resident would be a recruit for the *EPL*. More than likely, they would put one in her room and one in Brian's again since Joyce was already working here. It just made extraction easier.

Outside, in the center courtyard, the spring night air had a bite to it, but Dot didn't care. It was her last night on Earth.

She had loved Chicago. She had loved watching the seasons here through the windows over the last twenty-plus years.

But she wouldn't really miss it.

A moment later the yellow light from above took her and the lieutenant up into the transport ship.

Lieutenant Sherri helped her into the coffin-like sleep chamber one last time and stepped back and saluted.

"It has been an honor to serve you, Captain," she said.

"The honor has been mine to serve with you," Dot said. "See you in about fifty years."

"That's a promise I'll hold you to, Captain," Lieutenant Sherri said, then closed the lid to the sleep chamber.

She did her standard two taps to tell Dot it was secure.

And a moment later Dot was asleep.

THIRTY-THREE

April 28th, 1962
Equivalent Earth Time
Location: Deep Space

ONCE AGAIN DOT awoke from the deep sleep and pushed the lid to her coffin open, reveling in the feeling of being young again.

After being in that old body, this just never got old.

Her skin was smooth, her hair full and brown and not brittle.

And her legs worked.

She levered herself out of the coffin and landed on her feet, enjoying the feeling of standing on them without worrying about falling. And without the aches that came with trying to walk.

She stripped off her old-lady nightgown and tossed it back into the coffin. She wouldn't need it again. But she would let someone else throw it away.

Back on Earth, her son would be getting a phone call that she had passed away easily in her sleep. He would be upset, but her leaving would make life easier on him and his children. There was a lot more money in her estate than he knew about, and that would surprise him.

She just wished she could see his face when he discovered that.

She would miss him and her grandchildren, she had no doubt. But she would survive.

And so would they. That was the nature of death.

But she wasn't dead. She was getting a chance to be reborn in a brand new home, and that had her excited.

She got her uniform out of the closet and got dressed, enjoying the feel of the silk blouse and the photon stunner on her hip.

She looked to be in her mid-twenties this time and she assumed she was at Steven's Base. But she wasn't sure. This was clearly her cabin on *The Blooming Rose*. So no telling exactly where she was.

But now she got to stay in this young body, not go back to the old, crippled body.

This was the body she remembered.

Finally ready, she opened her door and stepped into the hallway.

There were people on both sides of her door.

Everyone snapped to attention and saluted.

She laughed at first, smiling and looking for Brian. This had to be his doing, but she didn't see him.

She saluted back and then everyone broke into cheers, welcoming her.

Marian Knudson from Brian's ship stood next to Steve and both Dot's crew and Brian's crew were mingled and cheering and shouting welcome and congratulations on the coming marriage to her.

Then from down the hall she heard a loud "Attention!"

Everyone stopped and again snapped to attention, holding their salutes.

Through them came the most handsome man she had ever seen, making an entrance from an old Hollywood movie.

Once again the sight of him just took her breath away.

Captain Brian Saber stopped in front of her and keeping a strictly military face, also saluted.

All she wanted to do was shout and jump on him, but somehow she managed to hold herself together, staring at the man she loved more than she could ever imagine loving anyone.

Finally, letting him hold his salute just an extra second or so, she saluted back.

Brian snapped off his salute and said with a smile on his face to everyone in the hallway, "As you were."

Everyone went back to cheering as he said simply to her through the noise, "I love you."

Then she kissed him and felt him kiss her back and felt his wonderful, strong arms around her.

And she knew she was home.

NEWSLETTER SIGN-UP

Be the first to know!

Just sign up for the Dean Wesley Smith newsletter, and keep up with the latest news, releases and so much more—even the occasional giveaway.

So, what are you waiting for? To sign up, go to deanwesleysmith.com.

But wait! There's more. Sign up for the WMG Publishing newsletter, too, and get the latest news and releases from all of the WMG authors and lines, including Kristine Kathryn Rusch, Kristine Grayson, Kris Nelscott, *Fiction River: An Original Anthology Magazine, Smith's Monthly,* and so much more.

To sign up go to wmgpublishing.com.

ABOUT THE AUTHOR

Considered one of the most prolific writers working in modern fiction, *USA Today* bestselling writer Dean Wesley Smith published far more than a hundred novels in forty years, and hundreds of short stories across many genres.

At the moment he produces novels in several major series, including the time travel Thunder Mountain novels set in the Old West, the galaxy-spanning Seeders Universe series, the urban fantasy Ghost of a Chance series, a superhero series starring Poker Boy, and a mystery series featuring the retired detectives of the Cold Poker Gang.

His monthly magazine, *Smith's Monthly*, which consists of only his own fiction, premiered in October 2013 and offers readers more than 70,000 words per issue, including a new and original novel every month.

During his career, Dean also wrote a couple dozen *Star Trek* novels, the only two original *Men in Black* novels, Spider-Man and X-Men novels, plus novels set in gaming and television worlds. Writing with his wife Kristine Kathryn Rusch under the name Kathryn Wesley, he wrote the novel for the NBC miniseries The Tenth Kingdom and other books for *Hallmark Hall of Fame* movies.

He wrote novels under dozens of pen names in the worlds of comic books and movies, including novelizations of almost a dozen films, from *The Final Fantasy* to *Steel* to *Rundown*.

Dean also worked as a fiction editor off and on, starting at Pulphouse Publishing, then at *VB Tech Journal*, then Pocket Books, and now at WMG Publishing, where he and Kristine Kathryn Rusch serve as series editors for the acclaimed *Fiction River* anthology series.

For more information about Dean's books and ongoing projects, please visit his website at www.deanwesleysmith.com and sign up for his newsletter.

For more information:
www.deanwesleysmith.com

ALSO BY DEAN WESLEY SMITH

THE SEEDERS UNIVERSE

Against Time

Sector Justice

Morning Song

The High Edge

Star Mist

Star Rain

Star Fall

Starburst

COLD POKER GANG MYSTERIES:

Kill Game

Cold Call

Calling Dead

Bad Beat

Dead Hand

Freezeout

Ace High

Burn Card

Made in the USA
Monee, IL
25 June 2020